Navajo Long Walk

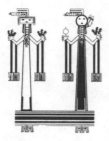

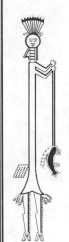

Navajo
Long Walk

Nancy M. Armstrong
Illustrations by
Paulette Livers Lambert

ROBERTS RINEHART PUBLISHERS
IN COOPERATION WITH
THE COUNCIL FOR INDIAN EDUCATION

International Standard Book Number 1-879373-56-4
Library of Congress Catalog Card Number 94-66493

Published in the United States of America by
Roberts Rinehart Publishers
Post Office Box 666, Niwot, Colorado 80544

Published in Ireland by
Roberts Rinehart Publishers
Main Street, Schull
West Cork, Republic of Ireland

Distributed in the United States and Canada by
Publishers Group West

Contents

The Council for Indian Education Series

The Council for Indian Education is a non-profit organization devoted to teacher training and to the publication of materials to aid in Indian education. All books are selected by an Indian editorial board and are approved for use with Indian children. Proceeds are used for the publication of more books for Indian children. Roberts Rinehart Publishers copublishes select manuscripts to aid the Council for Indian Education in the distribution of these books to wider markets, to aid in the production of books, and to support the Council's educational programs.

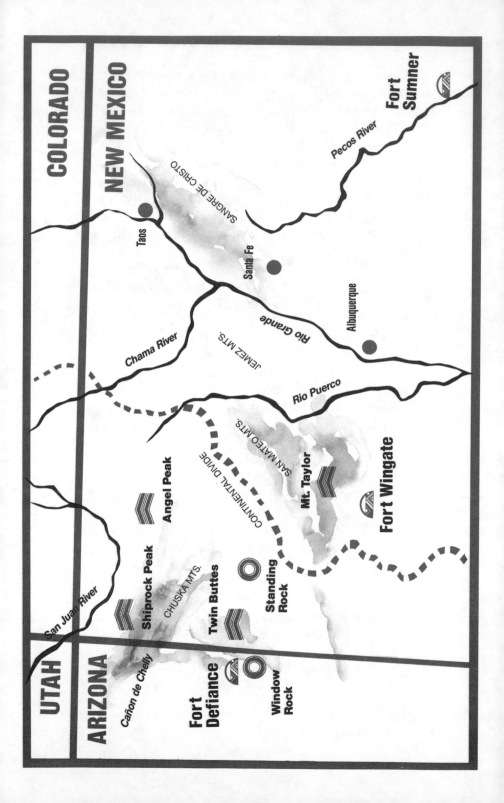

Introduction

In the early 1860s, the United States government was under pressure from ranchers, farmers and other Indian tribes in Arizona and New Mexico to put a stop to raiding by the Navajos. In 1863, although the Civil War was in full force, Union Army forces returned to confront the Navajos.

The army decided they must be moved to a reservation and assimilated into the American way of life. An area known as Bosque Redondo on the Pecos River in eastern New Mexico was chosen as the site of Fort Sumner and the Navajo reservation.

Knowing the Navajos would not go voluntarily, Colonel Kit Carson was sent to wage a campaign that would force them to surrender. It included the destruction of crops, livestock and hogans. The campaign was helped considerably by Col. Carson's successful march through Canyon de Chelly in the bitter winter of 1863–64.

Although some escaped capture by hiding in the inaccessible caves and canyons of Navajoland, more and more Navajos surrendered in 1864, and about 8000 made the "Long Walk" to Bosque Redondo. The forced march of 300 miles from Arizona into New Mexico and four years of confinement at Fort Sumner is remembered bitterly to this day.

1

A peace treaty signed on June 1, 1868 between the United States government and the Navajo returned to them a portion of their homeland—3.5 million acres set aside along the New Mexico-Arizona border.

The story of these difficult years, the Long Walk and four-year confinement, is told through the eyes of Kee, a Navajo boy, and his family. The family's love for each other and their animals, and the strength and resilience of the Diné (The People) is vividly portrayed.

Chapter One

Trouble Comes to the Mesa

Through the smoke hole in the top of the hogan Kee could see that sun-bearer was just beginning to light the sky, yet his father, Strong Man, was already eating his breakfast. Kee's grandmother, Wise One, was talking with him in low tones as they ate. He must be going raiding again, Kee thought. Oh, how he hoped Strong Man would find Kee's mother, Gentlewoman! The hogan had seemed so lonely without her these last two years since she was captured and stolen away by the Utes. Strong Man had spent much time riding with other Navajo men, trying to find her. If that should happen, it would be the happiest day of Kee's life.

As Kee stretched under his worn sheepskin, Strong Man smiled down at him and said, "My son, take good care of the sheep and your sister and grandmother while I am away. I will try to bring back a horse from this raid. It is time you had a horse of your own." A broad smile crossed Kee's face. He could hardly contain his excitement. He knew the Navajo called horses "that by which men live," and he dreamed of having one of his own.

At the sound of approaching hoofbeats, Kee quickly rolled out of his sheepskin. His uncle, Red Cloud, burst into the hogan and said to Kee's father, "Come, we must travel fast. There's trouble. Soldiers from Fort Defiance have captured some Navajos and taken them to the fort."

As Strong Man and Red Cloud galloped away, Kee's little sister, Hasba, crawled from her bed of sheepskins and they began their breakfast of corn meal and goat's milk.

"Why should soldiers be attacking the Navajos?" Kee asked. "Why can't they just leave us alone?"

Grandmother shrugged her shoulders. "It is the way of soldiers," she said. "No one can tell what they will do. We hope that they will not come this far, but keep your eyes sharp today as you herd the sheep and goats."

"Maybe we should just stay here today," Hasba suggested. "It sounds dangerous to be out there."

Kee's laugh was somewhat forced. He tried to sound confident as he said, "The sheep and goats have to eat. But don't be afraid little sister, I will be with you."

"Just don't go farther than you have to. Don't go trying to show how brave you are," Wise One said. "And take Small Burro with you."

Kee nodded his head and forced a little smile. Then as he and Hasba came out of the hogan to begin the day's work, Gray Dog jumped up from under a juniper tree, bounded to Kee for a good morning pat, then raced ahead to the corral. Kee and Hasba let down the poles across the corral gate, and sheep and goats poured out to be herded across the mesa to the water hole.

Hasba let down the poles across the burro's corral and clicked her tongue at Small Burro. "Come along, lazy one," she shouted.

The donkey made no move. Soon Wise One was at the gate clicking her tongue. Small Burro was up and running to nuzzle Wise One's shoulder. "How can he tell your clicking from mine, Grandmother?" Hasba asked.

Wise One laughed. "I have been talking to him that way since the day he was born. He knows he is mine." She scratched his ears and said, "Go along with you now." Small Burro trotted after the sheep.

During the long days of herding, the children had to find their own fun. In the late afternoon a goat walked past where Kee was watching the sheep. He knew this goat was a bit mean if teased. Yet he stood up and pushed the goat just to see what it would do. Lowering its head, the goat wheeled in anger. Kee ran. Seeing the goat chasing Kee, Hasba ran toward the goat. It stopped chasing Kee and ran toward her. She jumped aside, the goat ran past, then quickly turned and chased the pair of them.

The children tried to run to Small Burro. If they could mount the donkey, the goat would leave them alone. But the goat was smart, and kept between the children and the donkey. So they ran toward the hogan. Soon they reached a low hill with rock outcroppings. They crawled into a hole in the rocks. The goat climbed up to the opening and tried to bite the children's feet, which were sticking out. Yelling and kicking, Kee tried to make the goat go away.

At the sound of a horse's hoofs, the goat left and Kee and Hasba crawled out of the hole. A white man in a blue uniform riding a beautiful horse laughed down at them.

Kee had never seen a United States soldier, yet he knew the man was one because Strong Man had told him how the soldiers dressed. He was afraid more soldiers would be nearby. A soldier would not come into Navajo country alone. The Diné, as Navajos called themselves, were enemies of the soldiers.

The soldier pointed to the goat running in the distance. The children just stared at him until he rode away, still laughing.

Hasba began to cry. Kee said, "Do not be afraid. If we see more soldiers we will take Grandmother and some sheep and go to our cave in the canyon. We will hide there, and if the soldiers come, we will roll rocks down on them."

Kee did not feel as brave as he sounded, but he wanted to make Hasba less afraid.

Faithful Gray Dog had herded the sheep toward the hogan. Kee was happy to see that Small Burro had followed. Grandmother would never forgive him if something happened to her pet. Kee mounted the donkey and helped Hasba up behind him. He hurried the sheep.

Grandmother was waiting by the corral. "Did you see a soldier?" she asked. "He came to the hogan. He is looking for Strong Man, I think."

Kee wondered how Wise One could know the soldier was looking for his father. She could not understand white man's language.

The good smell of mutton stew greeted them when they entered the hogan. As Wise One knelt near the fire pit to dish it up, she said, "How I hope your father can find Gentle Woman on this raid and bring her back. Then he must stop fighting and raiding. All the Diné must. If we keep it up, we shall be dragged down the white man's road and only coyotes will live on the land."

Kee thought his grandmother was not wise to say such things. He could hardly wait until he was big enough to join the raids. How else could they get "that by which men live?" Other tribes stole horses from the Navajos. Should they be cowards and not try to steal some in return?

Chapter Two

Off to the Hide-out

Sleep would not come to Kee that night. He lay watching shadows on the wall made by moonlight shining through the smoke hole. Suddenly, he heard the sound of hoofbeats. He sat up in alarm, his heart pounding so hard it felt as if it would break his ribs. The horse must be bringing a soldier who would kill them or try to take them prisoner.

When Wise One heard the hoofbeats, she was up as swiftly as an eagle dives. She was lighting a torch at the fire pit when the door blanket was thrust aside and Kee's father rushed in.

Talking fast, Strong Man said, "The white soldiers think they are going to drive us to a place they call Fort Sumner. We will not go there! Gather the things you need but be quick. We must be gone from here before sun-bearer lights the sky. We will take some of our sheep and go back to our place in the canyon. Up there in the high country where we grazed our sheep all summer, it will be harder for the soldiers to find us. We should not have returned to our hogan so early."

Wise One went to the corral to fetch Small Burro to load him. Small Burro sighed, grunted, snorted, brayed, and in all the ways he knew, complained about having his rest disturbed. Wise One clicked her tongue, patted him, and let him know that she was sorry for him.

The sheep also complained with loud bleating as Kee hurried six of them out of the corral, along with a nanny goat Wise One wanted to take so they would have milk.

"What will become of the sheep we leave here?" Kee asked his father.

"I will come at night to take them to the water hole and let them graze. Gray Dog can stay. He will keep the coyotes away."

"Father, please let us take Gray Dog to watch the sheep in the canyon. We have only a brush fence there. He will keep them inside for us." Kee was thinking more about his dog's welfare than the sheep.

After a short silence, Strong Man said, "My son, your dog can go with you."

Kee headed the sheep and the goat in the direction of the canyon. Gray Dog would keep them moving together. Strong Man lifted Wise One up on Swift Runner as easily as if she had been an eagle feather, and swung Hasba up behind her. With Wise One holding the lead rope, Small Burro walked beside Swift Runner, coaxed along by the clicking of Grandmother's tongue.

Kee and his father followed on foot. Strong Man said, "I am sorry there is no horse for you yet. We did not go raiding. We met some Navajos camping close to Fort Defiance who told us the United States government has ordered all raiding to stop. All Navajos are ordered to surrender at Fort Defiance. Those Navajos who had surrendered to save their herds, wanted us to do the same. But we will never surrender."

Wise One moaned. "The day will come, my son, when we must learn to live in peace."

Strong Man laughed. "We will disappear as we always have. The soldiers will soon get tired of searching for-

Navajos. We will go on raiding and will grow rich from the spoils of our enemies."

Kee soon found it impossible to keep up with his father's long strides. Strong Man waited for him. "Up on the horse you go. We can travel faster if you ride." He lifted Kee up in front of Wise One. Hasba was already asleep with her head resting against her grandmother's back.

Sun-bearer was beginning to light the sky when Strong Man's family reached the bottom of the trail leading from the mesa to the canyon. Gray Dog growled and stopped the sheep. Strong Man signaled Wise One to stop the horse and donkey. Kee could hear the rustle of leaves in the grove of cottonwood trees they had entered, and the water in the small stream nearby. He felt sure Gray Dog could hear more.

Two Navajos stepped from behind a tree. "Ai," Strong Man gasped. "You gave me a fright."

The men laughed. One said, "Had you been of an enemy tribe or a white man, we would have given you more than a fright. We allow only Navajos to enter the canyon. Many have come tonight."

The family went on. Red sandstone walls grew higher on each side. Other Indians, gathering corn and peaches at the garden patches, exchanged a few words with them. At their own garden, Kee and Hasba picked and ate peaches from low branches while Wise One gathered a few ears of corn. Strong Man grew impatient. "Come, let us hurry along to our cave."

They did not stop at the brush hogan beside their garden. They went on across the stream and climbed up the side of the canyon to the cave hidden between two tall red rocks.

At the foot of the cave, Kee helped Wise One unload

Small Burro. Grandmother told the donkey what a fine fellow he was to be so much help. When everything was on the ground, Small Burro rubbed his head against Wise One's shoulder as if to tell her all was forgiven. Then he trotted off to rest in the shade of some cotton-wood trees.

The sun was overhead, and the coolness of the cave felt wonderful after the climb over the rocks to reach it. In a small room at the back of the cave, useful things were already stored: dry wood, dried corn, and piñon nuts from last year's crop.

Wise One made a fire in the pit, and soon they enjoyed a meal of corn meal. Then they curled up on sheepskins and slept the day away.

Darkness arrived early in the canyon. Strong Man left on Swift Runner to care for the sheep on the mesa. Wise One and Hasba rode Small Burro and Kee walked beside them to the garden where they picked corn, beans, and peaches. They could not carry much, but Wise One said, "We will come every night until we have enough for the winter."

The next day while they shelled beans, stripped corn, cut peaches, and placed them on hot rocks to dry outside the cave, Kee wondered why his father had not returned before dawn.

That night, with Small Burro already loaded to leave the garden, Kee heard horses' hoofs stepping up the can-yon trail. Grabbing Wise One and Hasba, he pulled them into shadows cast by the brush hogan. When the horse and rider came close the family was relieved to see Strong Man, who was startled to see them step out from the shadows. Hasba and Kee rode back to the cave with their father, following Wise One on Small Burro.

It was easy to tell that Strong Man was upset. As soon

as they were in the cave, Wise One lit a torch from the fire pit and asked him, "What dreadful thing has happened?"

With great bitterness he said, "The sheep have been driven away from the mesa. Not only ours, but herds all over Navajoland. Corn crops have been burned. The soldiers do not aim to kill Navajos but to kill our crops, drive away our animals, and starve us into surrendering. We are to be taken to this place called Fort Sumner. What right has the white man to tell us where and how we shall live?"

Wise One sat down beside the fire pit, her head in her hands. For a short time it was quiet in the cave, then Hasba began to cry. Wise One gently cradled her in her arms. Rocking from side to side she said, "We are the Diné. Our ancestors lived in this land for hundreds of years. The white man cannot know how much we love our home of red rocks and gray desert within the circle of the four sacred mountains. It is ours. No good can come of driving us out."

Suddenly Kee was filled with hatred. White soldiers had taken their herd of sheep. They must find a way of getting revenge. "My father is right," he said. "We must never surrender."

Chapter Three

Soldiers Find the Canyon

Many families were hiding in caves in the canyon. Navajo scouts told them that white soldiers were often seen on the rim of the canyon searching for ways to get down the steep sides. Kee knew that farther up the canyon, trails known only to Indians wound around the steep rocks. It was possible to get out of the canyon on foot or horseback, but these trails were dangerous because they were so steep and narrow.

Food was scarce. Already frost had killed what crops were left in the gardens. Women of the same clan as Wise One came in the night begging for food to feed their children. Wise One told Kee and Hasba that sharing had always been an important part of their way of life. It had helped the Navajos as well as other tribes survive many hardships in the past. Kee was not surprised when she said that they must share as much of their food as they could.

It was not safe to let the animals out to graze where they could be seen from the rim. Each night Kee and his father went into the canyon to cut grass for them.

Finally, one by one, Strong Man killed their sheep. There were so few of them that they hated to see even one of them go. Winter was coming and it was cool enough so the meat would keep. They ate only small amounts so it would last as long as possible, and Wise One used the bones and marrow to make soup.

Gray Dog gnawed at what remained of the bones, and kept himself alive mostly by catching mice, pack rats, and chipmunks. Once Kee saw him catch a small black, tuft-eared squirrel.

When five of the six sheep had been eaten, the children knew the last one had to go. They ate only a little corn meal that day, with a few of last year's piñon nuts and some bitter juniper berries mixed in, and Kee knew that although his father never showed his grief, Strong Man's feelings about killing the last of the sheep were as strong as his own. Kee watched as Hasba put her arms around the sheep, talked to it, and cried into the wool on its neck. Kee stood by, showing no emotion. He was glad his father did not see the tears that trickled down his face. When he was helping Strong Man skin and dress out the sheep, he noticed that Hasba was nowhere to be seen.

The goat ate any dry grass and brush Kee could find for it, but it got thin and quit giving any milk. When all the mutton was gone, the goat had to be eaten, too. Although some winters in the canyon were without snow, it snowed often that year of 1864, adding to the misery of the hungry Navajos.

Late one night, the scout, Long Earrings, came to Strong Man's cave to warn him that Kit Carson, with four hundred soldiers, was setting up camp at the west mouth of the canyon. The canyon had two branches and Long Earrings asked Strong Man to ride up one branch while he rode up the other. "Tell the people to put out their fires in the daytime, hide any animals they have, and keep out of sight."

After Strong Man rode away, Wise One said, "Kee, go and bring Small Burro into the cave."

Kee called Gray Dog from the back of the cave to go with him. He said to his grandmother, "Do not worry. We shall all be safe here together."

Wise One sighed. "Safety is not much use, child, if we are to starve."

Strong Man did not return that night. Hasba cried because he was not there when she awoke. "He is hiding today. He will come tonight," Kee said. "Do not be afraid." But Strong Man did not come that night either.

The following day, when afternoon shadows were filling the canyon, the three in the cave saw soldiers and mules floundering through snow toward the west end of the canyon. White soldiers had somehow discovered a way in from the east end, and were on their way to join Kit Carson at the west end.

The path along the stream bed was covered with thin ice. At times the mules' hoofs broke through the ice. The animals rolled and struggled to keep their footing. Men slipped and fell. Watching from the cold cave, Kee laughed at their struggles. He could tell from the way Wise One made soft little clickings with her tongue that she was sorry for the white men. He wondered how she could be. They were the cause of all their troubles. Then, to Kee's great surprise, he saw many Navajo men, women, and children, following the soldiers. They were surrendering! Kee could feel only contempt for them.

Chapter Four

Time to Surrender

 The following morning was gloomy, threatening more snow. Strong Man had not returned.

Wise One brought their only sack of dried corn from the storage space at the back of the cave. She gave each of the children a small handful for their breakfast. She gave Gray Dog a smaller handful, then searched out a few corn husks for Small Burro. She sat and looked sorrowfully at the children as she slowly chewed her small portion of the hard corn. Then she folded their sheepskins and blankets and laid them across Small Burro's back.

"Where are we going?" Kee asked, but Wise One did not answer. Kee worried as he helped her carry their few belongings out of the cave and stack them neatly near Small Burro. He understood why his grandmother would feel that they must now try to escape from the canyon, but where would they go? There was no safer place. He wanted to ask again, but he knew she would not talk until she was ready.

Finally, she sat on a rock ledge just outside the cave and, holding her thin arms out toward Hasba and Kee, she beckoned them to her. Hasba ran and sat on her grandmother's lap. Kee followed and tried to read his grandmother's eyes as he waited quietly for her to speak.

Finally, Wise One reached out and took his hand. "We

18

are going to the white soldier's camp. To make peace with them is the only way left to us."

Kee stiffened and pulled away. "No, Grandmother. No! We can't do that. Father would be very angry!"

Hasba cried. "We cannot leave here, Grandmother. Father will not know where we are. He will not be able to find us."

"He will find us, little one. He will know there is no other place for us to go. Let us start now before more snow comes."

Wise One tied her cooking pot and water jug on Small Burro's back, and carried the sack of precious corn herself. Kee guided the donkey over the rocks down to the trail. "You could ride behind the things or Small Burro," he said to his grandmother.

"No, it is enough for him to carry our belongings. He is too weak to carry me, too."

Upon reaching the garden patch, they were horrified to discover all their peach trees had been cut down. The day before Kee had heard chopping sounds echoing along the canyon walls and decided the soldiers must be gathering fire wood. Now he saw they had been destroying the peach trees, another way of starving the Navajos into surrender, and making sure they did not try to come back.

Wise One walked among the fallen trees looking as if she had just lost many good friends. Kee could not look at her unhappy face. Anger rose up within him. He held back. He wanted nothing to do with the cruel soldiers. How could they do this to people who had done them no harm? He wanted to drag Grandmother and Hasba back to the cave, to run away and try to hide in the mountains, anywhere. He was sure Wise One must hate the soldiers as much as he, but he also knew she would say it was better to cooperate with them than to starve or freeze alone in the mountains.

Wise One walked on to the brush-covered summer hogan. Mice had built a nest inside, away from the snow. Gray Dog was happy to discover them. Small Burro pawed the ground finding a few soggy cornstalks under the snow, but the family found nothing they could use.

Walking was not difficult since the snow had been trampled into a trail by men and mules the day before. Before they saw the soldiers' camp that dark, stormy afternoon, they could smell meat cooking. Kee's stomach churned, and growled. He looked at Hasba, and their steps quickened a little. Then Hasba stopped, saying, "It is the white man's food. They will not give us any."

Kee's heart thumped as they neared the camp. He knew Hasba was afraid also. If Wise One felt fear she did not show it. They were almost to the first tent when a Navajo they knew by the name of Many Goats appeared. "Greetings, Wise One." he said, "You show wisdom in coming here. Where is Strong Man?"

"Long Earrings asked him to take messages to our people. When he is finished, he will come to find us."

With all his heart, Kee hoped what Wise One said was true. He was afraid his father had been killed by white soldiers, or had gone away from Navajoland rather than surrender.

Many Goats said, "Come with me. I will take you to Colonel Carson. Do not be afraid. He treats kindly the Navajos who surrender. I will tell you what he says, and will tell him what you say."

"You are a smart man to learn the white man's language," Wise One said.

"Someday all Navajos will learn it, I think," Many Goats replied.

A look of scorn crossed Kee's face. To himself he said, "Here is one Navajo who will not learn the white man's ugly language."

Colonel Carson was not big. He would scarcely have reached Strong Man's shoulder. In a quiet voice he spoke to Many Goats, who then said, "Colonel Carson is glad you have come. He hopes all Navajos will come. He want us all to gather at Fort Defiance. There we will be fed until plans can be made for us to go to Fort Sumner, which will be our new home."

Kee thought, "He only asks us to give up our home and our way of life. How would he feel if someone asked the same of him?"

What kind of meat Strong Man's family ate that night they could not tell. Most likely, it was horse or oxen stewing in the big vessels on the campfires. They were given their fill of the tough meat with a bit left over for Gray Dog.

The tired family rolled up in their sheepskins on the ground, between two tents. Wise One rested with her head on Small Burro's side. He was stretched out full length soaking up the warmth of the fire. Gray Dog curled up with Kee. The boy ached with longing for his father. He strongly felt the Diné, a proud people, should not be sleeping at the white man's fire.

Chapter Five

Back to the Mesa

Kee was still sleeping soundly when the shrill notes of a bugle startled him to his feet. Small Burro jumped up dumping Wise One's head on the ground. Gray Dog barked. Hasba screamed and clutched Wise One. They were not the only ones to jump in fear. Navajos who had been in camp a few days laughed at all the frightened ones, telling them the cause of the harsh sound and helping them to laugh at their fears.

Many Goats shouted to the Navajos to gather in front of Colonel Carson's tent. He told them what Kit Carson said: "You Navajos must go to Fort Defiance where you will be fed and receive warm blankets. I am going there now with a few of my soldiers. You are to follow us. I know those of you who have no horses cannot travel as fast as we can. I trust you. Set your own pace. Navajos who do not come to the fort will be hunted until they are all destroyed."

Walking with Wise One and Hasba back to the tree where Small Burro was tethered, Kee thought about his father. Strong Man knew many good hiding places in different parts of Navajoland. Carson's men would have a hard time finding him, unless he had already been killed before he was able to escape from the canyon.

Wise One said, "We will not hurry after the soldiers.

23

I know the way to Fort Defiance. When we were young, your grandfather and I went there to camp. After the white men made the fort, we were told to keep out of the green meadow there or our sheep and horses would be shot. We never went there again."

The Navajos began following the soldiers out of the grove to the narrow trail that led up to the canyon rim. A soldier stood at the beginning of the trail, handing each Indian a chunk of dried meat. When Kee received his piece, Gray Dog stood up on his hind legs, pleading with his large, dark eyes. Kee broke off a small piece for him. The soldier reached into his bag for a chunk and threw it on the ground. A surprised expression crossed Kee's face. If he had not seen it, he would never have believed a white man could be so kind to a dog.

Before long, more than two hundred Indians were strung out in a long line following the soldiers. Sun on the canyon rim had melted much of the snow. Small Burro foraged along the sides of the road. Kee kept wishing Wise One would say, "We will turn off at our hogan," but she walked in silence. Gray Dog began ranging in the direction of the hogan. He would stand a long distance away, head thrown back sniffing, then circle back to Kee. After the dog had done this several times Kee said, "Grandmother, let us go and look at our hogan. Perhaps we shall find some food we can use for our journey."

Wise One smiled. "All the way I have been wondering whether or not we should visit our hogan. Now you have all decided for me."

Then Small Burro turned off the road in the direction of the hogan with Gray Dog beside him. Gray Dog was puzzled by the absence of sheep. He ran in and out of the empty corral looking for them. Small Burro waited pa-

tiently at the hogan until he was unloaded, then trotted into the brush shelter in his corral. He lay down with a sigh of contentment. He was home once more.

Soon a blazing fire made with dry wood found in the hogan, warmed them outside. Corn meal mush with bits of dried meat Wise One had saved warmed them inside. "Grandmother," Hasba said, "Please let us stay here where we can be happy and where Father can find us. I do not want to go to the white man's camp."

"None of us want to go, little one. You will find as you go through life you must often do things you do not want to do. A few days here and we would be without food. Your father is not ready to surrender to the white man. He will not come back here. We will stay one night. Kee, get the ladder your father made." She pointed to the top log on the wall. "I seem to remember hiding some sacks of corn there."

Kee found three small buckskin sacks. One held dried corn, one dried peaches and the third piñon nuts.

Too soon for all of them tomorrow became today. After stretching and yawning loudly, Wise One said, "Go and bring Small Burro to the hogan so we can load him."

Wise One and Hasba had the blankets and sheepskins folded and the packs ready for each to carry when Kee pulled aside the door blanket saying, "Grandmother, Small Burro will not come. I have coaxed and threatened him but he will not budge."

"Is anything the matter with him?" Wise One asked.

"Not that I can see. He is standing, but he will not leave his shelter."

"He wants me to coax him." Wise One put her head out of the hogan and clicked her tongue. "Come along, little bad burro." Then she set all their belongings outside the hogan ready to load. Still Small Burro did not come.

Grandmother went to the shelter followed by the children. As soon as she was close enough, Small Burro nuzzled her arm. She scratched his ears and rubbed his muzzle. "Now come along, bad boy, we are in a hurry." Small Burro braced his feet. He would not move.

Kee said, "Of all the stupid animals, a stubborn burro is the stupidest. Gray Dog would never act like that."

Wise One walked out of the enclosure and picked up a stick. She shook it in front of Small Burro. "Come out of that shelter or for the first time in your life I shall beat you." She tugged at the rope.

The donkey moved his long ears back and forth, rolled his eyes, but did not budge. Grandmother walked back and whacked Small Burro on the flank as hard as she could.

The children's mouths flew open. They were as surprised as the donkey. Before Wise One could drop the stick and get hold of the rope, Small Burro trotted out of the shelter to the hogan and stood still to be loaded.

All morning, as they trudged along the road, Wise One held Small Burro's lead rope. She kept telling him what a fine burro he was. She pointed to bits of grass poking through the thin layer of snow and waited for him to eat them. He occasionally nuzzled her shoulder to let her know she was forgiven.

Chapter Six

On to Fort Defiance

 When afternoon shadows began to lengthen, Wise One pointed to a clump of piñon trees away from the trail. "We will camp there for the night," she said.

Kee hunted pieces of bark and twigs to start a fire. Soon they were warming themselves as they rested on sheepskins. Gray Dog had his head against Kee's leg. Suddenly he threw his head back and sniffed, then dashed away through the trees. Anxious to see what Gray Dog had scented, Kee ran after him.

When he came to an open space away from the trees, Kee saw Gray Dog had killed a rabbit and was about to tear it apart. The boy knew the dog was hungry and he hated to take the rabbit away from him. But they were all hungry. Kee shouted at Gray Dog. With one paw on the rabbit the dog looked up, then bent his head again to tear at it. Kee shouted angrily, "Get away." Tail between his legs, Gray Dog slunk away. Picking up the rabbit, Kee hurried back to camp. The dog followed at a distance.

On seeing the rabbit, Hasba clapped her hands. Wise One found her knife and knelt to skin it. Kee could see his dog lying some distance away watching. "Grandmother, Gray Dog caught the rabbit for himself. I took it away from him. He is hungry, too."

Wise One stood up. Pushing Kee's black hair away from his forehead, she said, "He is a good dog. We will give him his share of the rabbit."

At dawn the next morning the little family was walking again. About the middle of the afternoon they came out on the brow of a hill overlooking the valley where Fort Defiance stood. They gazed down on a group of log and adobe buildings, a collection of old mud pigsties, and corrals filled with hundreds of sheep.

As they started down the long hill, Gray Dog began to whimper and run ahead of the family. "Call him back, Kee," Wise One said. He is itching to herd those sheep. He may get into trouble." Two soldiers with guns were walking up and down near the corrals.

Kee shouted at Gray Dog. The dog returned, whimpering and running in circles around Kee. The boy put down the things he was carrying. He took the dog's head in his hands. "I know how you feel about the sheep. Someday we will get some sheep again for you to herd. Now stay with me."

Hasba said, "I wish we could tell which are our sheep. They were our friends. In those big corrals they all look alike."

"I hate the white man for stealing them." Kee told his grandmother.

"Hate will not bring back the sheep," Wise One said. "Hate can do nothing but hurt the one who hates."

On the way down the hill they stopped to talk with several family groups who had set up camp. A few had tents supplied by the army. With the large number of Navajos arriving daily the supply had soon been exhausted. Some Indians had made brush shelters. Others camped on open ground with only blankets or pieces of canvas for protection.

Wise One asked each group if anyone had seen Strong Man or heard what happened to him. No one knew anything about him.

A chilly wind began to blow by the time they reached the bottom of the hill. Wise One was anxious to find a place to camp before the winter day ended. Opposite the fort parade grounds she saw a narrow wash. A few families were camped at the opening. Leading Small Burro, she skirted around the campers and went into the wash until she came to a scraggly little juniper tree growing sideways out of the bank. She tied the donkey to the tree and began to unload. "We will be warmer down here in the wash than on the hill. It will protect us from the wind."

Bugle notes sounded through the chill winter air. A woman called up the wash, "Old One, that is the call for us to go to the fort for food. Bring something to carry it in."

Wise One carried two flat round baskets when she and the children lined up with other Navajos on the parade grounds. At the doorway of an adobe warehouse where supplies were handed out, a soldier dumped a dipperful of white stuff into one basket. Another soldier dumped a dipperful of red beans into the other, and a third soldier handed Kee a small slab of bacon. Wise One gave Hasba a basket to carry. "What is this white stuff, Grandmother? Is it to eat?"

Kee put a pinch of it in his mouth. He spit and spit. "It is poison, I think."

A woman behind Wise One spoke. "No, it is not poison. It is flour. The white people use it all the time. A soldier told us to mix a little water with it and cook it in thin cakes on a hot rock. It does not taste good but it is something to eat."

The bone-weary family reached their camp. Kee held a little of the flour on his palm for Gray Dog. The dog turned his head away. "It must be poison, Grandmother. Gray Dog has too much sense to eat it. Shall I dump it out?"

"No indeed, child. No food should ever be wasted. Tomorrow I will find a way to fix it. Tonight I am too tired to think." Wise One gave each of them a little food from the sacks she brought from their home. Spreading the sheepskins behind a blanket hung from the juniper tree, the three lay down close together with the rest of their blankets over them.

Chapter Seven

A Happy Surprise

The next morning, Kee saw a Navajo digging with a shovel he had obtained at the fort. Kee had never seen one before, having always used a pointed stick to dig around the corn. He borrowed the shovel and marveled at how much dirt it would hold. He and Wise One dug a hole in the hard bank of the wash behind the juniper tree. It took a long time, but they dug far enough to get their sheepskins inside. By stretching a blanket over the opening, they had a shelter from winter storms.

Each day saw new arrivals at the fort. Kee went among them, asking each family about his father. None had seen him or heard anything about him.

As the days began to lengthen, the cold grew less severe. With Gray Dog, Kee helped to herd sheep for the Navajos who were lucky enough to bring some to the fort. Being used to vast space with miles between hogans, they disliked the cramped conditions around the fort. They were happier when they could be away with the sheep.

One night Kee was awakened in the dugout by something touching his face. Thinking it was Gray Dog, he said, "Lie down and go to sleep or go outside."

He heard a chuckle, then a quiet voice said, "I am not Gray Dog. I am your mother, Gentle Woman."

Kee sat up quickly. He had to be dreaming. Yet someone's arms were tenderly holding him. He couldn't see his mother sitting beside him but he knew it was no dream. The feeling of her gentle arms was real. He buried his face on her shoulder and hugged her.

Though she scarcely remembered her mother, Hasba cried with happiness. Crawling to her mother's lap, she patted her face and stroked her hair.

Wise One pulled back the blanket over the opening to let in a little moonlight. She did not seem surprised at seeing Gentle Woman. "You are very thin. Are you hungry now?" she asked.

"I am too excited and happy to feel hunger now. Tell me all about Strong Man."

Wise One told her that Strong Man left the cave in the canyon and they had not seen or heard about him since. "My son is a proud man. He will not come unless he is captured."

Kee could see tears shining on his mother's face. He asked, "How did you find us, Mother? How did you escape your enemies?"

Gentle Woman said, "Let us all lie down together under the blankets and I will tell you what has happened to me since I was taken away from you."

Hasba cuddled into her mother's arms as she began her story. "We can be glad, Kee, that you had a sore foot and could not go herding that day. You might have been captured with me and sold into slavery. Six Ute horsemen surrounded me."

Kee spoke up, "When it began to grow dark that night, Father went looking for you. At first he could not believe it was raiders because even though the sheep were scattered, none had been stolen."

"These Utes were in too big a hurry to bother with

sheep. They had plans to meet Mexican slave traders on the mesa above the Hopi villages."

"Were the Utes mean to you?" Wise One asked.

"I knew it was no use to struggle. I was tied on a horse so I could lean forward and grasp its mane. They rode fast and long, stopping only to let the horses rest and to steal one more woman herder and her daughter. Sun-bearer was almost ready to leave the sky the next day when we reached the mesa. Mexican slave traders were already camped there. The smell of mutton cooking made us ravenous, we were so hungry. We were fed and allowed to rest while the Utes and Mexicans haggled over how much we were worth. I could tell the Utes were anxious to get away. After all, they were in Hopi country. There was also the chance Navajos would follow and get back their women."

Wise One told her, "Many raids were made to find you. Always Strong Man came home sad."

"I was not with the Mexicans long. As soon as payments were made the Utes took off on fresh horses. That night the Mexicans put us all under a large piece of canvas with guards resting outside on the edges.

"The territory we were in was familiar to me. As you know my mother was part Hopi. When I was a child we lived and herded our sheep not far from the Hopi village of Oraibi. My mother even taught me a little of their language. I thought if I could only escape, perhaps the Hopis would help me get back to you. Waiting until I was sure everyone was asleep, even the guards, I worked my way carefully out from under the canvas."

Hasba hugged her mother tightly. "How scared you must have been."

"I was so afraid I think I stopped breathing. I crawled on my stomach at first, then when I thought they could no longer hear me, I ran. I felt the safest thing to do was climb higher on the mesa and find a place to hide. I found a thick stand of juniper trees. Among the trees grew sagebrush and yucca. I tunneled under a clump of brush, pulling it around me so I could not be seen. I hardly noticed how badly I was getting scratched I was so frightened and so anxious to be hidden."

"Did the Mexicans come looking for you?" Kee asked.

"I am not sure but I think so. I strained to hear and thought I heard horses' hoofs and men's voices in the distance. Later, I could tell by the warmth under the brush that sun-bearer was high in the sky. I knew the Mexicans would have left for their own safety and I fell into a heavy sleep. It was dark when I woke up. I was hungry and thirsty. I broke off some pieces of yucca blossom stems to chew. Afterward I felt better and started to walk. I wanted to reach Oraibi because that had been my mother's village.

"Gray streaks of light told me sun-bearer was on his way back when I realized I was on the mesa where the village stood. Then I was afraid the Hopis would not be friendly. I sat down against a large rock and tried to remember the Hopi words my mother taught me.

"Before long a girl came out of the village carrying a forked stick. She was on her way to work in a cornfield below the mesa. I called a greeting to her. She took me to her father who was chief of the village. I made him understand that I was now his prisoner. 'Many times,' he said, 'Navajos have taken Hopi women and children for slaves. Now that you are here you will stay and work for us. If you do not try to run away we will be good to you. If you try to run away we will kill you'."

Wise One sat up. "For many moons I have been saying this stealing of animals and people from other tribes and

from white people must come to an end. There can be
no happiness until people learn to live in peace with one
another."

"Little Mother, while I was with the Hopis I thought
often of the many times you have said that. Now I think
the same."

Wise One yawned. Gentle Woman said, "I am tired,
too. Let us sleep. Tomorrow I will tell you the rest of my
story."

Kee lay under his sheepskin, thinking. "How weak
women are. They are willing to make peace even with
the soldiers! There is no peace in my heart. Father did
not give in. He must be out there somewhere enduring
the hardships, defying the soldiers. I am only a boy. But
someday I will be big enough and strong enough to join
him. Together we will prove that we can still raid the
tribes that had raided us. We will steal whole herds of
horses and sheep from them. In my heart I will never
give in."

On following days, Gentle Woman told her family
about life among the Hopi Indians. Though she was a
gifted weaver she did not weave while she lived with
them. Among the Hopi, the men were the weavers.
Mostly she worked in the fields. She was treated as one
of the tribe and could have been happy if only her family
had been there.

Gentle Woman said, "News came to the village that
white soldiers were hunting Navajos and wanted Utes
and Hopis to lead them to Navajo hiding places. When
I learned the Navajos were surrendering at Fort Defiance
to be taken to Fort Sumner, a long way to the east, I
knew I must escape or I might never see my family again.

"I hid a small buckskin bag under a rock in a field.
For many days I put bits of dried meat, corn and dried

berries in it. One dark night I left the village. Hiding by day, walking by night, I ate whatever shoots and berries I could find to make the food in the sack last. After many nights I found the fort. A soldier frightened me half to death with his gun."

"They will not shoot any Navajos," Kee said. "Kit Carson made that promise when we were at the camp near the canyon."

"Well, I did not know that," Gentle Woman replied. "I was afraid because I could not make the soldier understand I was looking for you. Then Long Earrings came where the soldier was guarding. He told me where I could find you."

Chapter Eight

The Long Walk Begins

One day Long Earrings came to talk to Kee. "Is your dog good at herding sheep?"

Kee looked proudly at his dog, and declared. "Gray Dog is the best herd dog in all Navajoland."

Long Earrings grinned. "I am sure you speak the truth. We will soon be starting on the long journey to Fort Sumner. It will be too far and too hard a trip for Wise One to walk. If you and your dog will help herd the army sheep on the journey, I can ask for a place for Wise One to ride in one of the wagons."

Kee bristled. "I am Navajo. I will not herd the sheep the soldiers have stolen from the Navajos! Grandmother can ride on Small Burro. I have promised Eagle Feather I will help him. A Navajo does not break a promise."

"These are difficult times," Long Earrings said. "We must learn to compromise. Eagle Feather has only a few sheep. The army has many."

"But he has no dog to keep them together. Besides, he is my friend."

Long Earrings shrugged as he walked away, saying. "But if we cooperate, the army's sheep will feed us along the way."

Covered wagons, each with a team of oxen were drawn up near the fort. Wagons bulged with sacks of flour, sacks of beans, sides of bacon, casks of water. They were so loaded down that only a few old people could ride. Some lucky Navajos still had horses to ride. Those having a few sheep and goats chose to walk with their grazing herd. Most of the Diné were on foot.

Early on March 6, 1864, the first caravan climbed slowly out of the valley at Fort Defiance to follow roads made by army ox carts. Thirty wagons piled with rations were followed by 2,400 Navajos, 400 horses, and 3,000 sheep.

Before starting the trek Gentle Woman said, "Our journey will be long. Let us try always to stay close together. Having each other is the most important thing in our lives. With so many people and animals it would be easy to lose one another."

Small Burro complained at being loaded again. Wise One walked beside him to gently soothe his hurt feelings. There was no room on him for her to ride.

The first day seemed very long to Kee. Though he and Gray Dog were kept busy herding Eagle Feather's sheep, he kept wondering how long the journey would take. Would it be too far for Wise One and Hasba to walk? What kind of place was it that they were going to? Would there be shelter there and enough to eat?

Finally, after a day that seemed like forever, they reached their first campsite. The wagons were drawn into a large circle. Navajos were herded inside the circle. Kee angrily eyed the soldiers who kept watch outside the circle, seeing that no one escaped.

The Diné shared what little wood they could find within their area and built fires to cook the rations handed out by the soldiers.

The next morning when Kee, Hasba, and Gray Dog went to help Eagle Feather get his sheep on the move they found him kicking and shouting at a ewe that refused to get up. As soon as Eagle Feather saw Kee he shouted, "Tell your dog to nip this sheep and get it started."

Running to the sheep, Hasba saw a tiny, newborn lamb nestled beside the ewe. She turned in anger to Eagle Feather. "Of course she will not leave her lamb."

"She will have to leave it," Eagle Feather replied. "The lamb is too little and puny to walk. It will not live anyway. She must come without it."

Hasba's eyes flashed. "It will live. I will carry it, then it's mother will come along."

Eagle Feather laughed. "All right, I give the lamb to you. Carry it if you like."

"Oh, sister," Kee said, "We have a long way to go. You get tired without carrying anything. Besides it is so puny it cannot live."

Hasba did not bother to answer. She already had the tiny lamb in her arms. The ewe quickly stood up. After nuzzling her baby she walked contentedly at Hasba's side.

By this time Gentle Woman and Wise One had come to see what was keeping the children. "Look Mother, look Grandmother, this lamb is mine. Eagle Feather gave it to me."

Wise One clicked her tongue. "The lamb is very weak but we will save it for you if we can."

"I will carry it all the way," Hasba said.

Gentle Woman shook her head. "My child, the lamb will be half grown by the time we get there, I think."

"It will not be good for you or the lamb to carry it," Wise One said, "Come with me." Walking over to Small Burro she rearranged the bundles on his back so there was a small empty hollow space in the center. When she

put the lamb there, it cuddled down happily. "Now the lamb is as safe as in a cradle board," she said.

Small Burro snorted as he looked at the ewe walking beside him.

Chapter Nine

The Long Walk Continues

On the third day of the walk, Wise One stood for some time looking over the landscape in all directions. She smiled. "We are not far from Bear Spring. I remember this country from when I was a child." Patting Small Burro on the flank she said, "You will find much good food here, my beauty."

The next day they reached the valley of Bear Spring. Wise One was surprised to find that the United States now had a cavalry outpost nearby, called Fort Wingate.

Word was passed along that there would be a stopover here to grease the wagons, repair harnesses, and replenish rations. The Navajos were allowed to spread out in the direction of the spring. Kee was happy to see that there were many pine, juniper, and oak trees here. As he gazed around, the faint red color in the surrounding mesas made him almost feel at home. While Gentle Woman made a neat camp, he gathered a stack of the abundant wood for their fires.

The days of rest came to an end all too soon, and the bugle blew once more. Kee had hoped they would stay at Bear Spring. His father could easily catch up with them there.

Hasba's lamb had gained enough strength to walk a short distance beside its mother. As soon as the lamb showed signs of tiring, she asked her grandmother to put it on Small Burro's back.

The long caravan traveled slowly eastward, progressing about fifteen miles each day. When camp was made within sight of snow-capped Mount Taylor, Wise One became very upset. Looking at the mountain's long slope she said, "That mountain is the southern sacred mountain. The sacred mountains were placed by the Holy People as boundaries for the Diné. Surely we will not be forced to live beyond them!"

Kee watched as Gentle Woman took Wise One into her arms and tried to comfort her, saying, "Little Mother, this is a dark night for the Diné. But morning will come and we will return to our homes. I know the spirits are not pleased when we travel farther. But it is not our fault; we are being forced to disobey them."

"The Navajo spirits have abandoned us, I think," Kee said.

Gentle Woman turned toward him. "My son, such a feeling can bring only unhappiness. We must keep songs of beauty and bravery in our hearts. Even though the time seems so very long, we must believe our misery will come to an end."

Kee knew misery for him would never end until he learned what had happened to his father.

As the Navajos and soldiers continued toward the Rio Grande the country became flat and drab. Walking should have become easier, but many had sore feet from the chafing of torn and worn-out moccasins. Kee and Hasba put what was left of their moccasins into a buckskin bag on Small Burro's back and walked barefooted.

On a warm spring afternoon, the people saw cottonwood trees lining the west bank of a large river. They shouted to each other with joy, and pushed forward to

reach the shore of the Rio Grande. Spring runoff had
begun and the river was wide and deep. Kee stopped
high on the bank and stared in amazement. Gray Dog
dashed past him and ran into the water, wading out belly
deep to cool himself and lap water to quench his thirst.
Kee and Hasba both dropped the things they were carrying and dashed forward. How good the cool water felt
as they waded in the shallow edge of the river with the
other children. Women came to the shore and Kee saw
their smiles as they filled their cooking pots and water
jars.

Although sun-bearer was a long way from completing
his journey across the sky, orders came for heads of families to come to the supply wagons for rations and to
make camp for the night.

Kee stood in their camp and looked across the river. "I
never knew there was a river so big," he told Hasba. "It
must be very deep. We could never cross it. I hope we
follow it so we will be near the shore all the rest of the
way."

Chapter Ten

Crossing the Rio Grande

Gray Dog nuzzled Kee into wakefulness before bugle call the next morning. It was barely light enough to see. A cold wind had arrived with the dawn. Already there was a great commotion among the animals and people. Oxen were being harnessed to wagons and lined up along the bank facing the river. Word was sent around that old people and small children would ride across in the wagons. Many of the wagons were nearly empty; supplies were low and would be replenished at Albuquerque.

Panic spread through the camp. Navajos did not know how to swim. Being at the mercy of soldiers with guns and whips, the people had no choice but to get across somehow.

Kee felt sick with fear. His mother said to him, "You are the man of our family. Take your grandmother to one of the wagons and find her a place to ride across while I pack our belongings."

"No, no," said Wise One, "I will go across on Small Burro's back. He will not go into the water without me to urge him. I must see he gets across."

"Kee or I could perhaps get him across," Gentle Woman replied.

Hasba began to cry. "How will I get my lamb across? She will drown and so will I."

49

"You had better worry about the children and our things. Let me take care of Small Burro," Wise One said. "He will only be able to carry me across."

"You are right, Little Mother," Gentle Woman said as she knelt to roll the cooking pot and water jar inside their sheepskins.

Kee helped her tie them into a tight bundle, and together they carried the bundle. Hasba carried her lamb. Wise One led Small Burro. Gray Dog followed closely.

They joined the crowd of Navajos walking toward the river. Grown-ups were talking loudly about the injustice of making the Diné cross a wide river when they did not know how to swim. Frightened children cried, babies screamed, sheep bleated, horses snorted and neighed, and soldiers cracked whips and shouted angrily.

A few wagons had already reached the other side. More were starting into the river. A sweaty soldier, who was whipping a team of oxen to force them into the water, stopped long enough to grab Hasba and her lamb. He tossed them into the back of the wagon on top of other screaming children. Then he forced some young boys standing nearby to hang on to the tailboard of the wagon.

Hasba screamed for her mother. Gentle Woman could do nothing to quiet her fears. The oxen were already dragging the wagon into shallow water. When it hit deeper water, the oxen had to swim and the wagon twisted and turned in the current. At times, the boys hanging on to the tailboard were completely under water. Watching, Kee felt sure he would die of fright if that happened to him.

Eagle Feather came running through the crowd. "Bring Gray Dog and help me start my sheep across. They are afraid of the soldiers and their whips."

Kee did not answer nor take his eyes off the wagon that was now being pulled up on the opposite shore. Gentle Woman nudged him, "Go with Eagle Feather," she said. "His sheep are used to Gray Dog. He will be able to get them into the river."

Gray Dog, with the help of the boys, had no trouble keeping Eagle Feather's small herd separated from other sheep and goats. When they reached the river, Kee could see Gray Dog was anxious to get into the water. He ranged back and forth forcing the sheep closer and closer to the river's edge. Suddenly he rushed the animal at the head of the group. It floundered into the water, and the others followed. Gray Dog ran to the back of the herd to see that none went astray. When the last sheep entered the river, he barked with joy while splashing into the water himself.

Kee watched anxiously. Could his dog swim where the current was swift? Twice he lost sight of Gray Dog's bobbing head as he swam close to the sheep. Time seemed long before the first sheep dragged itself up the muddy edge of the opposite bank followed by the others, and Gray Dog shaking himself vigorously.

Both boys let out a breath. "The sheep are safe," said Eagle Feather.

"Gray Dog did it," Kee said proudly. Then he hurried back to the place upstream where he had left his mother and grandmother. He could not find them. Many people and animals were milling around on the opposite shore. Fires had already been started to dry the clothes and blankets of cold, shivering Indians. He was looking at the wagons and animals crossing the river to see if could find them when a soldier grabbed him. He took Kee to a horse that was just stepping into the mud on the bank. Two Navajo women, holding babies in cradle boards, were on its back. The soldier placed Kee's two hands around the horse's tail and squeezed them to show he must hang on tightly. Then he slapped the horse hard on the flank. The horse jumped. Kee was dragged across the mud into the river. Gasping, coughing, and spitting whenever he was tossed above water by the swimming horse, Kee clutched the tail with all his strength. Up and down, under and above the water, he was tossed until the horse once more felt ground under its hoofs. As Kee was dragged through shallow water into mud, he let go, collapsing on the muddy bank. Gray Dog ran to him and began licking mud from his face. Then a Navajo man stepped into the mud and carried him to the nearest fire.

Gentle Woman and Hasba, still holding her lamb, found Kee at the fire. He smiled at them. "How did you get across, Mother? Where is Grandmother?"

"I was lucky," Mother replied. "I came across on horseback and held our bundle, so our things are safe. I'm afraid Wise One is still on the other side. She was trying to coax Small Burro into the stream when a soldier motioned for me to mount the horse and guide it across. I hated to leave her, but I dared not refuse the soldier."

Kee jumped to his feet, scanning the river and opposite shore. The group waiting to cross was no longer large. But he couldn't see Wise One or the donkey. Gentle Woman said, "I will inquire among the people here for her. You watch the river."

Kee screamed, "Look! There she is! He ran downstream along the bank, followed by Gray Dog. He had seen Small Burro's long ears and struggling head. The little animal was caught in the swift part of the current and was being carried downstream with Wise One clinging desperately around his neck. Kee could not run as fast as the stream was carrying them. Oh, if only he could swim. The Navajo men could only watch his helplessness.

Tears blinded him as he ran. He bumped into a soldier who was unyoking a team of oxen. He pulled on the soldier's coat and pointed to the river. "Help me! It's my grandmother."

The soldier looked where the excited boy was pointing. He saw Wise One bobbing up and down on Small Burro. The animal was fast losing his valiant struggle against the current.

Kee started to run again. The soldier threw off his coat as his long strides covered the ground to the river. Swimming with strong, swift strokes he caught the floundering donkey. Snatching Wise One from the burro's back, he swam ashore holding her in one arm. Kee ran to the spot where the soldier was carrying his grandmother out of the river. He wished he knew the white man's word for thank you. He would never again think all soldiers were bad.

The moment the soldier set Wise One on her feet she started to run along the bank calling, "Small Burro! Small Burro!"

Kee ran after his little grandmother. She finally dropped to the ground completely exhausted. Kee sat beside her. Putting his arms around her, he held her thin, wet shivering body and tried to comfort her. She burst into hard sobs. "Small Burro was old like me. He did not have enough strength."

Gray Dog licked tears from her face. Kee patted her cheek ever so gently. It was the first time in all his life he had seen his grandmother cry.

Sorrow was in many hearts as Navajos hunted lost children, old people, and animals that had been carried downstream by the current. Some sheep and goats were washed ashore and slowly made their way back to camp. Wise One watched, waited, and wished, but Small Burro was never seen again.

Rations were meager that night as many supplies were soaked. But the Indians were very happy to learn that they would leave this hated place in the morning and travel north to the town of Albuquerque where they would rest and replenish supplies before going on to Fort Sumner.

Chapter Eleven

A Restful Stopover

The next morning, Wise One was so stiff and sore she could scarcely help Gentle Woman tie up their bundles. Kee hoped he could find her a ride. As he and Gray Dog were looking for Eagle Feather to help him with his sheep, he passed the soldier who had rescued his grandmother from the river. The soldier was loading supplies into the back of a wagon. Kee stopped, wondering how he could ask the soldier for a ride for Wise One.

Before he could try, the man smiled and asked him a question in English.

Kee shrugged his shoulders and stared at the soldier. The man made a swimming motion, then made the outline of a small person with his cupped hands. Next he sat on the tail gate of the wagon. Kee felt sure the soldier was telling him his grandmother could ride. He nodded and smiled. Pointing back to the camp, Kee tried to say with gestures that he would go for Wise One and bring her back. The soldier nodded and motioned for him to go.

At first, Wise One refused to go to the wagon. "No, child. I can walk and help carry our things. Hasba will need help with her lamb when it gets too tired to walk with the ewe."

Hasba said quickly, "Grandmother, if you ride you can hold my lamb when she is tired."

"Little Mother," Gentle Woman said, "When you are not holding the lamb, you can hold the bundle. If you ride, you will make it easier for all of us."

Wise One held out her hand to Kee. Gentle Woman watched them go, then said to Hasba, "Your grandmother will do anything that will help one of us."

The road to Albuquerque was only a rutted trail made by oxcarts along the eastern bank of the Rio Grande. Clouds of choking dust were soon stirred up by the marchers feet.

Upon reaching Albuquerque, the soldiers herded the families into a large corral by the river where all could camp together. Kee's swollen feet were bleeding, but he limped all over the corral looking for his grandmother. Suddenly, loud bells startled him. A Navajo told him the bells meant ration time. Kee worked his way through the crowd gathered around a supply wagon. He was thrilled when finally he reached the wagon and saw Wise One helping the soldiers hand out big loaves of bread.

Kee took a loaf of the bread back to camp. He was certain he had never tasted anything better. "Where did they make the bread?" he asked when Wise One came back to their camp.

"A Navajo who speaks some English told me that soldiers were sent to town before we got here to buy it. He said that Mexican women baked it in huge outdoor clay ovens."

Wise One went on and told them of other things she had heard while riding with the old ones in the wagon. "They say that we will stay many days in this camp. The soldiers will give us sheepskins to make new moccasins.

The wagons will be filled with enough food to last until we reach Bosque Redondo, which is a land of plenty. There, we will be given hogans and herds of sheep and some horses of our own, and we will also have land of our own to plant."

Gentle Woman shook her head. "Let us not believe these stories until we are herding the sheep given us. So many promises the white man has made have not been kept."

Wise One reached out and patted Gentle Woman's hand. "I know, I know. But it makes us happy to dream of such things."

"Anyway, we have one small lamb to start our herd," Hasba said.

"And a beautiful little creature she is, too," Wise One replied.

Kee hoped that some of the dreams would come true. He felt good now, resting his tired feet in the corral the Navajos named "The Place of the Bells."

Days of rest and better rations refreshed the Navajos. They started toward the Pecos River with more hope. Riding in a bumpy wagon with other old people was easier for Wise One than walking. She always found her family when camp was made at night. So did Kee and Gray Dog. He did not want to stay with Eagle Feather and his sheep at night.

Soon the land became endlessly flat. One day Eagle Feather said to Kee, "I do not like this country. There are no mountains, no mesas, and there is no color in the land. Day after day everything looks the same. We do not seem to be going anywhere. We might as well be standing still."

"Well, you should not expect any place to be as beautiful as Navajoland," Kee replied.

At fifteen miles a day, the column took many days to reach the valley of the Pecos River where at last, they saw the adobe buildings of Fort Sumner. The United States flag waved from a tall pole on the parade grounds. The river, narrow compared with the Rio Grande, ran past the fort. Cottonwood trees and salt cedar grew on both banks of the river. These trees had caused the Spaniards to name the place Bosque Redondo, "Round Grove." The Navajos had reached the end of the long walk.

Chapter Twelve

Arrival at Fort Sumner

 An officer and six soldiers rode out from the fort to meet the Navajos and give instructions to the men leading the column.

The magnificent gray horse the officer was riding took all of Kee's attention. The horse's gait thrilled him. Never had he seen a horse move with such grace and ease. When the officer reined to a stop, the horse stood motionless as the rock spires of Navajoland. Kee worked his way through the crowd to get as close to the horse as he dared. This was the kind of horse he had always dreamed of having. He turned away. He knew he was dreaming impossible dreams. But he would never forget this horse. He would remember and go on dreaming of someday owning such a horse. There could be no greater happiness.

The tired travelers were herded toward a large adobe-walled corral. The corral had been built as a gathering place where the Indians could be counted and given ration tickets. A man stood on the top of the wall to count them as they walked through the opening. Soldiers with bayonets stood on each side of the gate to hurry them along. Kee saw the frightened looks on the faces of his family and he tried to look brave, to make them feel secure. But he felt more like a frightened child than a protector.

61

The man ahead of them called out to Long Earrings as they passed him, "Why are we being forced into this corral? Are we to be penned up like sheep?"

"Don't worry," Long Earrings called back. "This is the only way the army can learn how many Indians they must feed and supply with tools. When we are all counted, they will let us camp outside the corral."

As the people went back through the gate, each family told a soldier the father's name. Long Earrings translated it and another soldier wrote it down and gave the family a ration ticket. When Gentle Woman received hers, Long Earrings told her, "Be sure you take good care of it. You have to have it with you when you go to the fort to receive food."

As they walked past the adobe barracks built for the soldiers, Kee asked his grandmother, "Where are the hogans you said would be built for us?"

Wise One shrugged her shoulders. "I think there is a mistake, child. I have looked up and down as we walked here, but I see nothing."

"Perhaps that is good," Kee said. "Maybe they will not keep us in this ugly place for a long time."

Now they would have to find a place to camp, just as they had while traveling. No shelter of any kind had been provided for the Navajos. Strong Man's family walked about a quarter of a mile downstream and a short distance away from the river to set up camp. It was an unhappy time for everyone.

Kee walked to the river and brought back a bucket of water for drinking. When his mother tasted it she spit it out and made a face. "We can't drink that; it's bitter."

"About as bitter as being held prisoners and ordered around by white soldiers," Wise One answered.

"And being away from our own hogan and red rock canyons," Gentle Woman added.

Up and down the Pecos River from Fort Sumner, the United States government had set aside forty square miles for an Indian reservation. Each Navajo family was expected to make some kind of shelter near the fort. The rest of the land would be used for farming and grazing. But there were no materials to build hogans.

"What are we going to live in?" Gentle Woman asked. "There's no wood for hogans."

"I saw some people coming from the fort with tents," Kee said.

"Maybe we can get one," Gentle Woman suggested and she and Kee left immediately to try. But when they got to the fort, all the worn out army tents had been given away. Some Navajos had gotten pieces of canvas, but for Kee's family there was nothing.

The next morning soldiers came by giving each family a shovel.

"We can try digging a hole in the ground to make a hogan," Wise One suggested.

Hasba laughed. "We can pretend we are prairie dogs."

Kee looked at her in disgust. "Who wants to be a prairie dog?"

His anger helped him dig furiously for a few minutes. Then his mother and grandmother insisted he let them take turns digging. It was hard not having a father in the family. He had begun to believe that his father was dead. He tried to push the thought from his mind, but it kept returning. Surely his father would have found them by now if he were still alive.

When they were completely tired out from digging, the sandy sides of the hole began to cave in. Gentle Woman sighed, "It's no use to dig deeper. But this hole

will do if we can find something for a roof. Our blankets
are all in rags."

"If we had some poles or tree branches, we could cover
them with brush," Wise One said. "But we must have
something to hold up the brush."

"Hasba, let us see what we can find along the river
bank." Kee said.

Hasba tied Small Lamb's rope around a rock so she
could not follow. Gray Dog went with the children.
Walking toward the fort, they passed many Navajos
building makeshift shelters.

The children hunted along the river's edge, picking
up a few small tree branches. They watched some soldiers swimming in the river. One of the soldiers came
out of the water toward them. Gray Dog growled as he
placed himself between the soldier and the children. Kee
recognized the soldier as the one who had saved his
grandmother from the Rio Grande. He put his hand on
Gray Dog's head, speaking quietly to him. The dog
stopped growling.

The shivering soldier picked up his heavy coat from
the river bank and threw it around his shoulders. "How
is the Tiny Grandmother?" he asked, making a sign for
a small person.

Kee recognized that he was talking about his grandmother and his face lit up.

The soldier smiled back and motioned for them to
follow him. Kee had to almost drag Hasba along as he
followed the soldier.

Hasba had tears in her eyes. "Let us run back to
Mother."

"He is the one who saved Grandmother. He will not
hurt us."

When they came to a building where the soldier lived,

the soldier put his hand on Kee's shoulder and pointed to the ground where they stood.

"He wants us to wait here," Kee told Hasba when the soldier went inside. Hasba wanted to run away, but Kee held onto her hand and said, "Wait."

The soldier came back out carrying a large piece of canvas. Kee smiled and thanked him in Navajo. Once more he wished he knew the white man's words for "thank you," but he was sure the soldier understood.

As the children walked away, Kee looked back. The soldier was watching and raised his hand in a farewell gesture. Kee returned the gesture, and hurried toward the dugout.

Chapter Thirteen

Kee Meets Smoke

Held down by rocks, the canvas proved a good roof for the dugout. The next day Kee and Gentle Woman grubbed out weeds and brush to cover the canvas. Hasba helped Wise One gather grass from which her grandmother made rough mats to line the walls of the dugout. Now they had a place to sleep, with protection against the rains and strong winds that blew across the open plains.

Long Earrings and one of his friends walked by. They stopped to look at the shelter. Long Earrings told Wise One, "They are giving us a reservation—only ten miles along the river and four miles wide!"

Kee didn't know what a mile was. There were no such words in Navajo. "Is that big?" he asked.

"Big? Ha! It would be enough for no more than five families to raise their crops and their sheep back in Navajoland. And they think we can grow enough food for all the Diné on it!"

Soon the men were ordered to use the shovels they had been given to dig irrigation ditches from the river to the fields that would be planted to raise food for the tribe.

Gray Dog carefully herded Small Lamb to join Eagle Feather's little flock each day. "What a big herd of sheep we own," Kee said with bitterness. "A herd of one."

When the fields were ready for planting, Kee and Hasba spent many days with other children, helping to plant corn, wheat, beans, and pumpkins. The soldiers insisted everything be planted in rows. Kee could not understand why the white man always wanted things different from the Navajo way. They made a hole and planted seeds anywhere in the field.

By now most of the Indians were in rags. About the time the crops were planted, a shipment of bolts of material for clothing arrived at the fort. As soon as they were told it would be distributed, everyone hurried to the fort with the ration tickets. Kee went with his family. They were passing the officers' quarters on the way to the store when Kee saw the wonderful gray horse tethered to the hitching rail. He ran to the horse. Admiring the animal from all directions, he wondered if the horse would allow him to touch it. He was stretching out his hand to pat the horse's muzzle when someone said "Oh, so you like Smoke, too. He is the most beautiful horse at the fort."

Kee whirled around, expecting to see a Navajo. He saw the Mexican who interpreted Navajo for the soldiers. Kee smiled. "So that is his name. It is a good one. His color looks like smoke. Will he let me pet him?"

"I think so. I have never tried. He belongs to Captain Harris."

During Kee's lifetime, his father Strong Man, had owned many horses. Kee had learned to ride almost as soon as he learned to walk. He had a gentle, confident way with animals, and they quickly learned to trust him. He patted Smoke's neck, then slowly ran his small brown hands underneath the silky black mane. The horse twitched his ears and pointed them forward when Kee quietly spoke Navajo words of endearment to him.

"Smoke likes you, I think," the Mexican said.

When Captain Harris came out of the officers' quarters, Kee dropped his hands and backed away. Smoke stepped forward and nuzzled his shoulder wanting more attention. Captain Harris smiled at Kee, then began talking with the Mexican. The Mexican turned and told Kee, "He says he has been watching you through the window. He thinks you have a way with animals. He wants to know if you can ride. I told him all Navajo boys learn to ride very young."

Captain Harris spoke again to the Mexican. Again, the Mexican turned to Kee. "He says he needs someone to take care of Smoke, someone to feed, water, groom and exercise the horse when he is too busy. He wants to know if you would like to do it. There might be extra rations if you do a good job."

Kee could scarcely believe his ears. Imagine being with Smoke every day. It was the best thing that could happen, except, of course, to own such a horse and be free to ride him in Navajoland.

Captain Harris smiled down at Kee and talked to him. The Mexican translated. "He says he can see that you would like the job. He wants you to come to the parade grounds early tomorrow morning when there isn't a mob around like tonight. He wants to be sure you can handle Smoke."

As the captain walked back to his quarters, Kee put both arms around Smoke's neck, whispering, "You and I will be the best of friends, my beauty."

Happiness filled the tiny, dugout hogan that night. Wise One had received blanket strips large enough to make Gentle Woman and herself new dresses. Gentle Woman would make Hasba a new dress and Kee some trousers from the flowered calico.

Kee was not interested in woman-talk about new clothes. All he wanted was for morning to hurry and come so he could ride Smoke.

Chapter Fourteen

School Begins

Captain Harris had only to see Kee astride Smoke to know the boy could handle the horse. Kee soon began spending a good part of each day at the stables and horse corral. His happiest days were when he was told to take Smoke for a run.

Sometimes Kee was given a small bucket of milk to take to the dugout. His family would rather have been drinking goat milk from their own herd in Navajoland, but the cow's milk helped to stretch their scanty rations and they were grateful for it.

When Kee was not busy with the horse, he went to the fields to try to help the men plant the crops. Since he had no father he felt that it was his duty to try to do the job of a man as well as he could.

It was not many days before he came back to the dugout and reported that the corn was up and growing. By the middle of summer it had tasseled and the family's mouths watered as they talked of the fresh roasted corn they would soon enjoy. But before the ears were half mature, corn worms destroyed most of the crop. Then hail storms ruined most of the wheat. The Navajos shared what crops there were, but there was little to store away for winter use.

Gentle Woman paced back and forth, shaking her head, saying, "What will we do? We will all starve before spring."

"We will live somehow," Wise One assured her. "The Diné always have. Perhaps Captain Harris can give Kee some extra rations."

But Kee told them, "Even the soldiers are getting short on food. They say they have sent word to a far-away place called St. Louis for more supplies, but it is a long, long, hard journey for the wagons. It may be the middle of the winter before they arrive, even if the snows are not deep this year."

Officers at the fort divided the tribe into twelve groups. They chose twelve Navajo headmen as leaders of the groups. Each headman was asked to encourage his band to build an adobe village. But adobe houses were the way of the Pueblo Indians, not the Navajo. Besides, this land was not good for them. They could not feed themselves from it. Why should they build a village that would never become home? The villages were never started.

Indian men had been set to work finishing an adobe building at the fort. Now that it was completed, they were told it would be used for a school for Navajo children. Young priests were coming from Santa Fe to teach them to speak the white man's language. The headmen were asked to encourage Navajo parents to allow their children to get an education.

Strong Man's family was under the leadership of Ganado Mucho, "many cattle." He was one of the few Navajos who had a big herd and was able to bring most of it with him to Fort Sumner. At times he even sold animals to the soldiers for food. Gentle Woman shook her head when Kee told her this. "That is not the way of the Diné. He should share with his own people, not deal with the enemy."

"People do what they have to do to survive," Wise One said. "Some of them no longer keep the Indian ways."

Ganado Mucho went from one miserable shelter to another, talking about the school. When he reached Strong Man's family, they were sitting on the ground near their supper fire, dipping into a pot of mutton stew. Wise One invited him to join them.

Kee listened carefully as the headman talked about the school to Gentle Woman. "It will be a great help to the tribe if some of our boys will learn the white man's language. Life is so much easier if you understand what people are saying."

A worried expression crossed Gentle Woman's face. "But is it safe for our children to be shut up with strange, white men all day? What do you think, Kee?"

Kee swelled with pride. His mother had asked his opinion as she would have asked his father had he been there. Although he felt a little afraid about the school, he said, "My mother, we will be as safe there as anywhere else at this fort. I would like to learn the white man's words so I can know what soldiers say when I am working at the stables."

Hasba ran to her grandmother, "I do not want to go to school," she said.

Wise One drew the little girl down to her lap. "You don't have to go to school, I think. You can instead learn to cook at the hogan fire and herd sheep. And learn to card wool and weave it, if ever we can have sheep again and poles to make a loom. Kee can teach you the white man's language."

Ganado Mucho smiled. "That reminds me. At a meeting of the head men and the fort officers, we spoke about getting poles for looms so warm clothing and blankets can be woven before the worst part of winter arrives. The

army will send wagons to the mountains for poles and needed firewood."

Gentle Woman turned to Ganado Mucho. "Kee will go to the school. I will go with him until I see that it is safe."

Ganado Mucho nodded. "As many mothers as children will be there the first day, I think."

Picking up a tin plate of discarded mutton bones, Kee carried it to the back of the dugout where Gray Dog waited patiently for his supper. A shadow fell across the ground as Kee gave the bones to Gray Dog. He looked up to see Ganado Mucho smiling down at him. "Kee, I am happy you want to learn the white man's language. Many of our boys will not try because of their hatred for the white man. It is true I acquired my big herd of cattle by raiding, but those days are over. We will never survive as a tribe unless we learn to live in peace with the white man, for he is here to stay."

On the morning school began, Gentle Woman and Kee joined the large group of boys and mothers sitting on the ground in front of the adobe school building. A tall priest in a long black gown came out with the interpreter to tell the children to come into the classroom. Mothers crowded forward with the children, but were told to wait outside.

Kee felt a small sickness in his stomach as he walked into the classroom, but he was glad he did not give way to tears, as some of the younger boys did.

The children sat close together on long benches. The teacher held up white cards with black marks on them. He told them the white man's words for the marks. Then the interpreter told them Navajo words for the marks. The priest had the interpreter tell them, "I will teach you the white man's language. You will teach me the Navajo language. We will both learn."

School lasted only a short time that first day. The children, not used to being confined, laughed and shouted as they tumbled out into fresh air and sunshine, joining mothers who were now able to smile again.

Hasba ran to meet Kee and Gentle Woman when she saw them approaching the dugout. "Say a little of the white man's language for me," she shouted to her brother.

Kee laughed. "It is not that easy. Tomorrow I will bring you a white man's word."

Chapter Fifteen

Weaving Brings Happiness

The promised poles arrived at the fort. Ganado Mucho sent Navajo men to help Strong Man's family build a loom. They put poles in the ground to make a shelter where the women could weave. Kee and Hasba gathered weeds, brush, and tree branches to cover the shelter.

Gentle Woman and Wise One were given a small amount of wool at the supply warehouse. The towcards and slender stick spindle Wise One carried on the long walk were once again put to use. Hasba was delighted to hold towcards again. She had begun to learn carding before leaving the hogan on the mesa.

The spindle danced under Wise One's small. strong hands. Kee marveled at the swiftness of her fingers as she rapidly spun the wool into twisted yarn. He waited anxiously for her to burst into song as she always had when spinning at the hogan on the mesa. She remained silent. The dancing spindle caused him to recall the sings in Navajoland. He wondered if the Diné would ever again know such happiness.

Here in this alien land beyond the sacred mountains, the spirits had deserted them. There was no use in holding ceremonies for the sick. Besides, who could provide food for the great feasts to follow each day's ceremony? Here no one had enough to eat, so how could anyone invite friends or relatives to share with them? He could almost hear the voices of the singers chanting, chanting, chanting. He could hear drums. He could see dancers and smell good food cooking on campfires.

His mother's voice brought Kee back to the present. "You and Hasba go to the river and hunt some tree bark and roots that might darken the wool. I also need a bucket of water to heat the dye."

The family worked together until warm blanket dresses had been made for the women and Hasba. A blanket was made for Kee to wear around his shoulders.

Strong Man's family was lucky to have the warm clothing. Snow and sleet blew early across the open plains that first winter at the fort. Because of the crop failure, rations had to be cut. Sickness spread among the Navajos. Unhappiness at being so far from their beloved homeland caused old ones to give up in despair. Many died.

Early each morning, Kee lifted the corner of the canvas over the dugout and climbed out. Whether snow, rain, sleet, wind, or sunshine met him, he trudged to the fort. His one happiness was taking care of Smoke. His fondness for the horse grew each day.

Only a small number of boys faithfully attended school now that winter had come. For Kee, the hours passed quickly. After school, he ran errands for Captain Harris. With great patience, the captain explained what he wanted done. This extra contact with white people improved Kee's English. Captain Harris talked to Kee about his own son, Jeff. Kee soon understood that the boy lived with his mother in the place where the wagons came from with the supplies. It was many days' journey by ox team from the fort. Kee understood it had been many moons since the captain had seen Jeff. "He will be about the same age and size as you are, Kee," Captain

Harris said. "He writes me letters and tells me about his school and his friends. I miss him very much."

Kee could not understand all the words, but he understood the captain loved and missed his son. He loved and missed his father with an ache that grew stronger all the time. He would never tell any white man about his father. He still had hopes that Strong Man had escaped capture and was hiding somewhere in one of the many canyons in Navajoland, although Gentle Woman said it was more likely that he had been killed.

One morning at the stables, Kee's soldier friend who had saved Wise One and given him the canvas, pointed to Kee's shoulder blanket. "Would your mother weave me a blanket like that?"

Kee shook his head. "No wool."

The soldier took Kee to his quarters and showed him skeins of red and blue yarn he had ordered from St. Louis. "Can your mother weave this into a blanket?"

Kee nodded. He knew Gentle Woman would love the bright colors and be happy to do something for the soldier who had befriended them.

"Good," said the soldier. "When it is done, I'll send the blanket to my mother."

Gentle Woman's loom was seldom idle after that. Several soldiers sent for yarn. She wove blankets to send to their wives and mothers. Building a small fire in the pole shelter she wove even on the coldest days. A little meat or bread from the soldier's rations often found it's way to Gentle Woman's dugout. When bits of yarn were left over she was allowed to keep them. She hoarded them carefully, hoping some day to have enough to make a bright blanket for their own use.

Chapter Sixteen

Cold, Hunger, and Comanche Raiders

When at last spring arrived, the leaves began to bud, and once again birds sang in the cottonwood trees. A new feeling of hope spread among the Navajos. Hoping to grow more food this year, they worked hard at cleaning the irrigation ditches and planting crops.

But Fort Sumner had been built on lands belonging to the Comanche Indians. The Comanche now resented this and began raiding the north and south ends of the reservation.

"Why should they attack us?" Gentle Woman asked. "It is not our fault that we are here."

"How would we feel if the army moved the Comanche into Navajoland?" Wise One answered.

"We'd kill them," Kee said, bringing the point of his finger around his neck as if taking off a head.

"If we had weapons," Wise One reminded him. "Now we can't even protect ourselves."

The Comanche continued to steal sheep and horses from the Navajos, who were already poor enough. When the Navajos complained to the soldiers, they were told that the soldiers were too few in number to fight the Comanche.

"If they didn't use their soldiers to keep us penned up, they'd have plenty to fight their wars," Kee grumbled. He was happy when he heard that some young Navajo men had slipped away in the night and brought back some of the stolen horses. He only wished he had a horse of his own and was old enough to go on some of these raids.

Grown-ups took on the responsibility of herding the sheep. They were afraid that the children would be captured and stolen along with the sheep to be sold as slaves.

By early summer, Small Lamb had nearly grown into a ewe. Hasba renamed her Dawn Flower. When Kee made fun of the fancy name, Hasba said, "Well, I found her just as sun-bearer was coming to the sky. She is beautiful so she should have a beautiful name."

Dawn Flower stayed near the shelter with Gray Dog to watch her. Hasba was busy taking care of another small lamb. One of Eagle Feather's ewes had given birth to twins, and the mother would accept only one. Hasba was happy to receive the cast-off twin, and gave it the same watchful care she had given Dawn Flower. She coaxed Kee to beg a little milk each day at the cowshed for the lamb. Once he said, "I'm afraid Gray Dog will be overworked now with a big herd of two to watch. He will not know which sheep to follow."

As summer progressed and the corn and wheat grew rapidly under the Navajos' care, Kee saw smiles on Navajo faces and heard cheerful greetings from the Diné as they worked together. They were adapting, working hard, determined to make the best of a bad situation.

But then, in mid-summer, the corn worms struck

again. Crops failed. Gentle Woman and Wise One wept as they walked with Hasba and Kee along their rows of corn, picking the few ears half-eaten by corn worms.

Kee shook his head in dismay. "The soldiers think they are so powerful, why don't they fight the corn worms? It's a much worse enemy than the Navajo!"

Wise One nodded her head. "There are some enemies that neither white men nor Indians have learned how to fight. Maybe, someday."

"I think the spirits of this land do not want us here," Kee said. "Perhaps when we get back to Navajoland, our own medicine men and spirits will protect us again." When fall came, the reed bins that the Diné had woven to store their grain were empty. A feeling of hopelessness spread among the Navajos.

Kee reported to his family that some of the Navajos had slipped away in the night. "I heard them whispering together yesterday. They said it would be better to be killed by Comanche or sold into slavery than to live in this land that does not want them. I should have gone with them. Maybe I could have made it back home and joined Father."

"Your father is dead," Gentle Woman answered. "If he were alive, he would have come to us. He must have given up by now."

"Given up? Not Father! Not as long as he is free."

"Perhaps he is free—somewhere," Wise One answered.

A few days later, as Kee was exercising Smoke, he saw soldiers on their horses bringing in a group of men who were on foot. The soldiers had hunted down and were dragging back the Navajos who had escaped.

As winter progressed, the feeling of discouragement was even greater than the year before. On cold nights Kee and the family huddled together in the little shelter to try

to keep each other warm. Kee realized that without his work with Captain Harris's horse and the extra food and fuel he received, they might not have made it through the winter.

With the coming of the third spring, Navajos who had not died of hunger, sickness, or discouragement were unwilling to plant any more crops in the alkaline soil. Yet they were forced to plant again.

In spite of all the hardships Hasba always managed to stay cheerful. "She was so young when we came here that this is becoming a normal way of life for her," Kee told his mother. "If we stay here she will forget our canyons and our mesa. She will grow up not ever knowing how Navajos ought to live."

One morning after Hasba stepped outside to greet the rising sun, she hurried back in, overjoyed. Dawn Flower had given birth to a lamb. Now she had a herd of three sheep. She cared for them throughout the summer as carefully as if there were a hundred.

Kee was now speaking English quite fluently. He still couldn't see much sense in clocks when they had the sun, but he learned that white men's years had numbers. This was what they called the summer of 1867.

Even though he sometimes went hungry, Kee was growing rapidly, and the soldiers who worked around the stables were now treating him as a young friend. In spite of himself, he was beginning to enjoy being with them. He hated to admit that white soldiers, the enemy, were his friends, but he began to realize that they, as individuals, were not the enemy. Some of them hated being here almost as much as he did. They, too, were captives far from home.

One of them confided to him that the government was getting tired of trying to care for so many Indians in a place where food could not be raised. The cost of feeding them was enormous, yet there was never enough to satisfy their hunger. "If we are lucky we may all be going home some day," he said.

Yet fall came and there was still no sign of change. Winter came, the Navajos went hungry, and the Comanche continued to raid. With the Navajo men cold, sick, hungry, and discouraged the Comanches were able to steal many of the sheep, goats, and horses. Because there was not enough grass nearby for the animals and it was not safe to take them too far away to graze, much of their livestock died that winter. Meals often came from the tough stringy meat of an animal that had starved to death.

Chapter Seventeen

A New Friend

When the spring of 1868 arrived the resilience and optimism of the Navajos was strong. They were beginning to smile again.

One morning when Kee was feeding Smoke, Captain Harris called him into his office. The happiness in his voice was obvious as he told Kee, "My son is coming to visit me while my wife goes to Boston to see her mother, who is ill. He will come with soldiers bringing the next wagon train of supplies to the fort. I am glad you can speak English. You will be good company for Jeff."

Kee felt almost as excited as the captain. He had never seen a white boy his own age. He wondered if Jeff would like to do the same things as Navajo boys. One unpleasant thought crossed his mind. He hoped Jeff would not expect to take over the care of Smoke.

One day, a few weeks later, as he stood at the hitching rail outside officers' quarters, Kee shaded his eyes as he watched for the long-overdue wagon train to come into view. Captain Harris was worried. He wanted to know the second the wagons appeared so he could go to meet Jeff.

Dust rose in the distance. Waiting until he was sure it was wagons and not Navajos herding sheep back to the fort, Kee dashed to the captain's office. "Wagons come!" he shouted.

Captain Harris walked with long strides toward his horse. Kee ran ahead to untie the reins. He watched horse and rider disappear across the parade grounds into the dust. He could leave now and go back to the dugout but instead he decided to wait and have a look at the white boy.

Smoke returned to the parade grounds with Jeff bouncing up and down behind his father. Kee chuckled inside. "White boy is not much of a rider, I think."

After dismounting, Captain Harris handed the reins to Kee saying, "Jeff, this is Kee, the only Navajo boy here who has learned more than a few words of English. He takes care of Smoke and runs my errands. You two should become friends."

"Hello, Kee," Jeff said. "I have seen Indian boys of many tribes on the streets of St. Louis. I have never had one for my friend."

Kee shrugged. "I have never seen white boy before. I go now to put Smoke in corral." Kee mounted and rode swiftly away.

Arriving at the stables early next morning he found that Smoke was gone. Captain Harris had waved to him from the parade grounds where he and other officers were checking the ration tags of Navajos already lined up to receive food. Kee thought, "Jeff must have Smoke. I hope he treats a horse better than he rides. He might ride too fast over ground pitted with prairie-dog holes. Smoke could step in one and break a leg."

While he stood worrying about Smoke and wondering what to do, he heard a snuffling at his back and felt a familiar nuzzling at his shoulder. He whirled to face Smoke. The horse was saddled but riderless.

Jeff was nowhere to be seen. Picking up the reins, Kee started to open the corral gate. Smoke pushed his arm as if to stop him. Just then it occurred to Kee that Jeff might have been thrown. "The way he rides it could happen fast," he said to himself, and thought how terrible Captain Harris would feel if his son was hurt.

Smoke nudged him again. "All right, all right, beautiful one, we will go and find him."

Mounting quickly, Kee let Smoke have his head. The horse ran straight for the river. Kee would never have chosen that direction. He had been afraid of the water ever since that horrible day the Navajos were forced to cross the Rio Grande on the way to the fort.

The Pecos was neither as deep nor as wide as the Rio Grande. In the deepest part the water came only to the horse's belly. Yet Kee's heart thumped wildly. He held his breath on the crossing and sighed with relief when the horse was on dry ground.

After loping across the prairie a short distance, Kee saw a wash ahead. He felt sure he would find Jeff there. The wash was wider than Smoke could jump and was probably a deep one. No doubt Smoke had stopped at the edge so abruptly that Jeff was thrown over his head.

The wash proved to be not only deep, but a jungle of sagebrush, cacti, mesquite, and yucca. Kee walked Smoke up and down along the edge of the wash trying to find hoofprints where Smoke had come to a halt with Jeff. No luck. Dismounting, Kee tried to descend the wash but could find no way down between the thick brush. Sharp yucca thorns grabbed at his calico shirt and pants. He called Jeff. In the silence that followed his calls, he could hear only his own breathing and Smoke's snorting. Occasionally he could hear the horse's hoofs strike a rock as Smoke ambled along the edge of the wash. Climbing back to the top, Kee thought, "If Jeff is under that mess

of brush somewhere I will never find him. I had better go for help."

A short distance away Smoke was pawing at the edge of the wash. Kee ran to him. He called Jeff. A second later Smoke pricked up his ears. Kee knew the horse had heard something. He called again. A faint moan reached him.

Kee struggled through the brush in the direction of the moan. Half-way down the wash he heard it again, above him. Looking back up along the tangled thicket, Kee finally saw Jeff. He was spread-eagled on a huge clump of yucca that was growing through a thick stand of sagebrush. Kee fought his way toward him. The white boy's eyes were closed, his face scratched and bleeding. When Kee was as close as he could get to the heavy brush, he called to Jeff. The white boy opened his eyes; a faint half-smile crossed his face. "I've been praying someone would find me. I tried to pry myself loose until my back was torn to pieces."

Kee was too short to reach over the brush to get hold of Jeff. "Wait, I get rope."

He wormed his way back to the top of the wash. Smoke stood at the edge watching for him. Kee unwound the rope hanging from the saddle, then tied one end securely to the horn. Holding the other end, he went back to Jeff. "I will toss a rope to you. Hold it until I climb to the top again. Smoke will pull you off the yucca. Then he will stand still until you pull yourself out of the wash by holding to the rope."

Kee tossed the rope. It fell short of Jeff's hands the first time but the next time it fell across his body and he found it.

As soon as Kee was at the top again, he put Smoke in position to pull away from the wash. Cupping his hands to his mouth, he shouted, "We are ready to pull. It will hurt bad."

At Kee's command, Smoke pulled slowly forward. A horrible scream rose from the wash as Jeff was jerked off the yucca. Kee shuddered, knowing how much it was hurting Jeff. "Stop," the white boy screamed.

Kee stopped the horse, gently patting Smoke's face and talking softly so he would stand still. He was about to go back and try to help Jeff when he saw the white boy's head and arms appear above the wash. He ran to help pull him over the edge. At the top, Jeff let go of the rope and collapsed face down in the dirt. His shirt was in shreds, his back a mass of bleeding scratches. Kee knelt beside him. "Rest here. I will go to the fort. Your father will bring a wagon."

Jeff raised his head slightly. "Wait, Kee. In a minute I can ride Smoke."

Kee said, "I did not know a white boy could be so brave."

When Jeff stood up, Kee helped him into the saddle. "I will lead Smoke. I might hurt your back if I ride behind you."

"I'll lean forward so you don't touch my back. I want you to ride too."

As they rode slowly, Kee said, "Now I take you to my grandmother. She will put her medicine on your many scratches. It will sting but it will heal them."

"I guess I can take it," Jeff replied. "It can't hurt worse than yucca thorns."

Chapter Eighteen

Little Mare Enters Kee's Life

Kee stiffened with fear when they reached the river. He was glad the white boy could not see his face. Once on shore, he let his breath out quietly and turned Smoke downriver.

Gentle Woman was sitting on the ground weaving at her loom when the boys reached the dugout. On seeing Jeff's back, she shook her head sadly, telling Kee that his grandmother was down inside the dugout. Before Kee could pull back the canvas cover, Wise One's head appeared above ground. "Grandmother, this is the son of my captain. He is hurt. Will you help him?"

Wise One smiled and disappeared. Almost as soon as she was out of sight she reappeared up the wooden ladder carrying a clay bowl with ointment. She spread it gently on Jeff's back. Knowing how the ointment smarted, Kee watched the white boy. Though he winced and drew his breath between his teeth, Jeff did not cry out.

On the way back to the fort Jeff asked, "Do Navajos always live in homes like yours?"

Kee bristled. "In Navajoland we do not live in holes in the ground like prairie dogs. There we can get logs to build hogans."

"You don't like it here, do you?"

"No Navajo likes it here."

94

"After living in St. Louis, I kind of like this open country."

"We do not like this flat land that everywhere looks the same," Kee said. "Navajoland has mountains and mesas covered with pines and juniper trees. Our hogans are not muddy holes in the ground. There our sheep grow fat. Our corn ripens. In the bottom of our red rock canyon peach trees grow. Here is nothing."

"When I grow up, I want to be an explorer like Colonel Kit Carson. Then I'll come to see your country."

The boys had come close to the riverbank. Jeff said, "When my back is healed we can swim together. You'll be glad to know I swim much better than I ride. You won't have to rescue me from the river."

Kee was quiet for so long that Jeff asked. "Don't you like to swim?"

"I do not swim," Kee answered. "Where I lived before there is no place to swim."

After a long silence Jeff said, "Yesterday I watched you ride Smoke from the officers' quarters to the corral. You rode so easily you looked as if you were part of the horse. I've never had a place to keep a horse, and I'm a bit afraid of them, but I wasn't going to let you find out. So early this morning I asked a soldier to saddle Smoke for me and went out to practice riding." He chuckled a little. "You see what happened to me. But I just had to get back on Smoke after he dumped me, or I'd never have enough nerve to ride again." He waited for Kee to say something. When he didn't, Jeff said, "Look, Kee, I'd like to learn to ride like you do. You teach me and I'll teach you how to swim."

Kee was about to say, "I do not want to learn." Then the memory of the horrible day he forded the Rio Grande flashed through his mind. Had he been able to swim he might have saved Small Burro for his grandmother. "You will show me how to swim. We will help each other."

"It's a bargain, Kee, and we'll have fun doing it."

While Jeff's many scratches were healing, Kee found a place on the riverbank behind a growth of salt cedar where he could practice wading without being seen. He shuddered with fear each time he tried, even in water that came only to his knees. He persisted until he could force himself to wade in to his waist. The first day Jeff was able to go in the river, Kee mustered up enough courage to get wet all over. In a few days, Jeff had him swimming clumsily, then with more ease. Soon, Kee showed such enthusiasm he was able to coax a few other Navajo boys to take advantage of Jeff's lessons.

As Kee was on his way to the stables one morning he heard galloping hoofs behind him. He whirled around to see Ganado Mucho astride his big, black horse. The Navajo headman reined in beside Kee. "I stopped at your hogan to find you. Kee, our Comanche enemies are making more and more raids upon our horses and cattle and sheep. So we need more men and boys to help keep the animals closer to the fort. I know you are a good horseman. I have seen you on the captain's horse. Will you have time with your school and work at the stables to help bring some of the animals in each day before sunbearer leaves the sky?"

Kee's eyes shone. He was proud to be asked to do a man's work. "I do not have to work at the stables. I just like to be with Smoke. I have taught the captain's son to ride and will show him how to take care of Smoke. But what can I ride to bring in the animals?"

"You can ride Little Mare. She is one of my horses I

keep staked near my hogan. Do you know which one I mean?" Ganado Mucho asked.

Kee answered, "Yes, I know her." But he thought, "Ugh, that ugly little brown beast with the crooked white stripes down one side of her face."

Ganado Mucho must have noticed the boy's disappointment. He said, "I know Little Mare is not large and handsome like Smoke, but she is good with cattle."

Kee managed a half smile. "She is a horse so I will like her."

At first Kee compared everything about Little Mare with his ideal, Smoke. She was ugly; he was the most beautiful horse in existence. She had stubby legs and a rough gait; he had long graceful legs and the smoothest gait of any horse he had ever seen. But after riding Little Mare for several days, he began to admire her wisdom. She seemed able to outguess ornery animals and she soon had Kee convinced that she could have rounded them up by herself, she was that smart.

He began to look out for Little Mare's welfare. When work was finished he took her to the stables where he could find her a little hay. He improved her coat by grooming her with a brush and a currycomb. She kept one brown ear pointed forward and her head turned in the direction Kee was working on her. He talked softly to her as he worked. Before leaving her at night, he staked her with a long rope near the river where she could find something to eat.

One afternoon as Kee approached Little Mare to begin work, she raised her head and gave a whinny of delight. Kee ran to the horse, put his arms around her neck, and laid his face against hers. "That's the nicest greeting I have ever had. Smoke has never done that for me." The whinny became a daily greeting.

Now whenever Kee had time, he and Jeff took long rides together, he on Little Mare and Jeff on Smoke. Although Kee was sure he would never ride like a Navajo, Jeff was becoming a fair horseman and loved to ride. And for Kee, Little Mare was the finest of all horses.

Chapter Nineteen

A Big Surprise

One morning at the end of May, not only the bugle but the fort cannon shattered the quiet dawn. Kee rolled from under his sheepskin, pulling on his shirt as he ran in the direction of the fort. Along the way, Navajos were climbing out of dugouts, running from brush shelters or rolling out from under ragged blankets to hurry toward the fort. All had expressions of wonder on their faces.

Kee saw Jeff coming on Smoke. As soon as the horse was close enough, the white boy told Kee, "General Sherman and other officers came late last night. The cannon firing was a salute to them. They have come to talk about a peace treaty. Barboncito and Ganado Mucho and some of your other headmen are also at the fort. Hop astride. We can go sit underneath the window outside the council room and maybe hear what some of them say. But you'll have to tell me what the Navajos say."

Happiness surged through Kee. "There will be an interpreter, or how could the general and other chiefs understand each other?"

Hundreds of Navajos from all directions were converging on the parade grounds. Kee tethered Smoke to the hitching rail. The boys ran around to the back of the officers' quarters, along the narrow, wooden porch to the window of the council room, and squatted down to listen.

Kee whispered, "Barboncito is begging General Sherman to look at the burrows that are our homes. He wants the general to taste the nasty, bitter water of the Pecos. He asks him to watch the few sheep we have left trying to find a blade of grass in this bare land. He says this land does not like us, and neither does the water."

Kee's eyes shone with love when he heard the voice of Ganado Mucho pleading, "Let us go back where we can build hogans and live as men, not animals. We will live in peace. Only let us go home."

The long talks lasted three days. On June 1, 1868, a peace treaty was signed between the United States of America and the Navajo, allowing the Navajos to return to their home territory, that would now become their reservation.

To Kee, the days and nights of waiting to start their journey seemed to last forever. At last, army wagons were filled with provisions. The horses and sheep that had survived were rounded up by the Navajos who owned them. The Diné, so sad and silent during the four long years of captivity, began to talk and laugh and sing once more.

Excitement kept Kee awake most of the night before their departure. Many times he climbed the dugout ladder to lift a corner of the canvas. Each time Wise One would ask, "Is sun-bearer in the sky yet?" Kee smiled to know his grandmother was as anxious as he was to begin the long walk again.

At dawn, groups of Navajos began passing the dugout, ready to start when the wagons pulled out. Kee wanted to take Wise One to the wagons and find her a place to ride. "No," she said. "We will walk slowly because Hasba's three sheep must eat. I can keep up with you."

Kee wished to leave his white friend a token of friendship. When he told this wish to Gentle Woman, she insisted he give Jeff the only blanket she had been able to weave for themselves. "But mother, our others are nothing but rags. You will need the new one on the journey home."

"To show you are a friend to the white boy is a greater need." Gentle Woman replied.

Carrying the blanket, Kee hurried toward the fort. He had so hated being a prisoner, it was only since the signing of the treaty he had thought how much he would miss Smoke and Jeff. It was going to be hard to say goodbye.

At the stables, Kee went inside Smoke's stall. Tossing the blanket he was carrying over the side of the stall, he rubbed Smoke's muzzle saying, "This is the last time I will pet you, my beauty."

A voice behind him shouted, "Kee, I'm glad you're here. I was just going over to your place to say goodbye."

Kee pulled the blanket down and pushed it at Jeff while patting Smoke's neck. "Here is small blanket my mother made for you to take to your mother."

Jeff's face lit up. "Kee, that's wonderful. My mother never had an Indian blanket in her whole life. Now don't forget I'm going to be an explorer and I'll come to visit you someday."

"Will you bring Smoke?"

"You bet I will, if we still have him. Then you and I will ride together in the Navajoland you talk so much about."

Giving Smoke one last pat, Kee managed to say, "It's a bargain, Jeff." Then he dashed out of the stable.

Knowing he would be needed to help carry family bundles, Kee hurried toward the dugout, lost in thought. Suddenly a horse nickered behind him. He knew that happy sound. Whirling around, he faced Ganado Mucho riding his black horse with Little Mare on a lead rope.

Kee rushed to the little horse. "Do you want me to help drive the cattle on the way back?"

The headman shook his head. "No, it is more important t'..t you help your family, since you are the only boy."

Kee knew that was true but he was sorry. He would have liked to ride the mare on the long march.

"Get up on Little Mare," Ganado Mucho said. "You can take her to your hogan and I will go back to my animals."

"Why should I take Little Mare to our hogan?"

"So Wise One can ride her. Your grandmother is too old to walk so far. And you can take care of Little Mare because now she is yours to keep always."

Kee's mouth flew open but no words came.

Ganado Mucho laughed, then said, "Do not look so surprised. You have earned the horse for the work you have done for me. I know she will be happy with you for I have watched you two together."

Through tear-filled eyes, Kee looked at his little horse. The first one that was truly all his own. He wondered how he could ever have thought she was ugly. She was so beautiful and so intelligent.

Chapter Twenty

Homeward Bound

 The Diné laughed and sang as they trudged along, or rode in wagons or on horses. Many wore old, blue army coats. Some women had dresses made of the white man's bright calico. Some men had trousers of the same material. Blue-coated cavalry men rode as escorts to the company for protection against other Indian tribes, and to keep the Navajos moving until they reached Fort Wingate.

The first day's march was long. Dust caked on sweating bodies. Yet when they camped for the night Kee thought his grandmother looked younger than she had since coming to Bosque Redondo. She helped Gentle Woman prepare the meager supper. The only water they had was what they carried in their water jars, but they used a little to wash the caked dust from their faces. "It is good to be going home," Wise One said. "We have lived four years in that evil place. Lived on promises made by the white man that they would give us hogans and sheep. Now again they promise us sheep and goats to take the place of those Kit Carson's soldiers killed. What a happy thing it will be if it comes true. But we must make plans to work hard and take care of ourselves with our own efforts as we did before."

Kee wanted to say, "Before, we had a father to help

105

us." But he kept silent. He wondered if the others thought of his father as often as he did.

He looked forward to crossing the Rio Grande. Now that he could swim he could help Hasba and his mother and grandmother. When he finally stood on the river-bank, he laughed and laughed. Being July, the river had long since carried away the spring run-off. Only in the center was there a narrow current of water to swim. The rest was shallow enough to wade. The Navajo waded joyfully in to wash their tired dirt-caked bodies. They drank the muddy water. It tasted sweeter than the bitter water of their prison camp.

Grandmother ate only a little of her share of bread and beans that night. Kee noticed her eyes glistened with moisture. Gentle Woman put her arm around Wise One's shoulder, though she said nothing. Then Kee re-membered the sadness of the first crossing when Wise One's beloved Small Burro was washed downstream.

Summer evenings were long. After eating, Kee decided to hunt for a rabbit. A change of food might make his grandmother feel better. He called Gray Dog. Though the animal was getting old, and was tired after the long day's walk, Gray Dog seemed as happy as Kee to go away from the noise, dust, smoke, and crowds of the camp. No rabbits were hiding in the gullies they searched.

When shadows began to lengthen, Kee turned back toward camp. The first thing he saw was a prairie dog, sitting on its haunches a short distance away. Gray Dog saw it too. Though the prairie dog was swift in running toward its hole, Gray Dog was swifter. He caught and killed the little animal. Bringing it to Kee, he dropped it at his feet. Kee patted the dog. "You are a good one. I know you are hungry, yet you give your catch to me.

This will make grandmother happy. She has not tasted prairie dog since she left Navajoland."

They hurried back to camp. Dropping the prairie dog in Wise One's lap, Kee said, "Gray Dog brings you this."

Wise One smiled, though tears still shone in her eyes.

Gentle Woman skinned and cooked the animal. Small as it was, Wise One insisted everyone in the family must have a taste. Gray Dog chewed the bones.

The way home led again past Mt. Taylor, the sacred southern mountain. Now, every night when the Diné made camp, some of them found rabbits or prairie dogs to help stretch the short rations issued by the army. "We are once more within the circle of the sacred mountains," Wise One told them. "The spirits remember us."

When a slight red coloring appeared in the cliffs along the route, the Navajos knew they were at last nearing home. Once more they reached Bear Spring. They saw the American flag flying over nearby Fort Wingate and were told to make camp for a long stay. Their reservation was to begin just beyond the fort, but the boundaries had not yet been set, so they were to stay at Fort Wingate for a while.

The blue-coats went back to Fort Sumner. The Navajos were no longer prisoners of war.

"Now that we are supposed to be free, why do we stay here?" Hasba asked her mother. "Why can we not go to our hogan on the mesa? I want to take my sheep where there is a corral and more food for them."

"Try to be patient, Little One," Her mother replied. "The white man has many things to decide for us." She sighed. "Things will never be the same as before we went to Bosque Redondo."

Waiting for the free life to begin was hard. So many people and animals were crowded together, all of them wishing for the silence of vast space. Often the oxcarts bringing rations from Albuquerque were late. The Diné were hungry most of the time. They gathered seeds, roots, and herbs. They hunted rats, rabbits, and prairie dogs for food. When riding away from camp on Little Mare, Kee was sometimes tempted to take off on his own. He knew several families had sneaked away, and the soldiers from Fort Wingate made no attempt to bring them back. They were no doubt glad to be rid of them. Kee felt sure he could find his way to Fort Defiance and from there to the mesa hogan. But he also knew his mother and grandmother and sister looked upon him as the man of the family. He could not disappoint them by leaving them behind.

Chapter Twenty-one

Back to the Mesa

The Navajos moved on before the first snow fell. A few days later, they looked again on the log and adobe buildings, mud pig pens, and sheep corrals of Fort Defiance.

The Diné could not feast their eyes enough on the hills covered with juniper and pine trees, nor breathe enough pine-scented air. Strong Man's family found their hole in the side of the wash still there. All the time they were unloading Little Mare and unpacking their bundles, Kee complained. "My mother, why do we not go on? We will be allowed to go anywhere now. We can be at our hogan in less than two days' journey."

"I know, my son, but we do not know what we will find there. We have no food. With winter already upon us we cannot find any. How can we live on the mesa?"

"Let me ride Little Mare to our hogan. I will see how things are there and come back for the rest of you."

"No, my son, you are too young to undertake such a journey alone."

Wise One then said, "Let us all rest here until the first ration day. When we receive food for the week, let us all travel to see our hogan. We can return before the next ration day."

"Oh Mother, would you do that?" Kee asked with excitement in his voice.

Gentle Woman hugged the little old grandmother. "It is easy to see why you were given the name Wise One. We will go."

Ration day arrived. The Diné were not frightened by the high-walled corral that had been built at Fort Defiance. They crowded in, laughing and talking.

Ganado Mucho, standing on top of the corral wall, waved to Kee as he walked through the gate. Then he began to talk to all Navajos in a loud voice. "My kinsmen, remember we have made a promise to keep the peace. No stealing. No killing. You must all work. Come for your rations each week. In the spring, the government will give each Navajo a few sheep and goats to start your herds once more. A school will be started here at the fort as the white men promised in the treaty. Those of you who want your children to have an education, send them to the school. Now, go home and live in peace."

The next morning, when the first streaks of light were showing in the winter sky, Strong Man's family was already at the top of the hill leading out of the valley. They looked back down the hill. "I hope we never come back to this place," Hasba said. "I hate it."

"I could come alone on Little Mare for our rations if Mother would let me." Kee told them.

Gentle Woman patted Kee's shoulder. "My son, you are too anxious to grow up."

Little Mare was so loaded with the family's belongings and rations there was no room for Wise One to ride. Gentle Woman insisted on stopping often. She said it was to let the sheep graze in peace, but she kept watching that Wise One did not get overtired. Kee was unhappy when they stopped to camp. He was impatient to cover more ground so they would arrive at the hogan early the next day.

Snow had fallen a few days before. In the warmth of the sun it had melted from the mesa except under trees. Kee went to a pine tree to get a bucket of snow to melt, so Gentle Woman could cook some of the beef they had received. Under the snow, he found a few cones still filled with nuts. "Piñon nuts," he shouted.

Hasba and Wise One joined him in scraping snow from under the trees. After a meager supper, they sat near the campfire happily chewing piñon nuts and tossing the shells into the fire.

At daylight they were walking again. Shortly after midday, Gray Dog began ranging far afield, then returning to the sheep. At intervals he would stand still, throw his head, sniff in all directions and start ranging again. Kee called the dog to him. He heard excited rumblings in the dog's throat. "He remembers this place, I think," Kee said.

"I remember it too," Hasba said. "We sometimes brought the sheep here to graze." She pointed to a clump of juniper trees. "Behind those trees is the pile of rocks where we hid when the goat chased us. That day was the first time we saw a white soldier. Remember, Kee?"

Kee nodded, his heart pounding. "We are not far from the hogan now."

Wrinkling up her face, Wise One said, "If I did not know better I would say I can smell the sweet smell of piñon smoke. It is perhaps only that I would like to smell it."

"Little Mother, that is exactly what I have been thinking," Gentle Woman said. "But I must be dreaming."

Just then Gray Dog bolted. Soon, joyful barking was heard in the distance. Kee dropped Little Mare's lead rope and ran. As he broke into the clearing around the

hogan, Strong Man came running toward him, Gray Dog at his side.

Strong Man stopped and stared. Kee rushed to throw his arms around his father. Strong Man murmured, "My son, my son, you are here at last."

Kee was surprised to find himself thinking, "I am now as tall as my father's shoulder."

By this time, Hasba had her arms around Strong Man's waist. Gentle Woman and Wise One stood at the edge of the clearing watching. Tears were running down Gentle Woman's face. Strong Man looked up from hugging Hasba and saw her. Walking forward as if he could not believe his eyes, he took her tenderly in his arms. "I have waited for this moment forever, I think." Suddenly he turned around, swooped Wise One into his arms, spun around, and set her gently down on the ground again.

Everyone was talking and laughing at once. Little Mare was unloaded and admired by Strong Man. She was led to the corral to be fed, to enjoy a well-earned rest, and make the acquaintance of Swift Runner.

Chapter Twenty-two

Home at Last

The hogan was clean. Sacks of piñon nuts stood against the wall. Strips of venison were drying on the wall logs. A fire burned in the pit. A large pot of mutton stew stood nearby, ready to warm. Sheepskins were spread around the fire to sit on. After looking around, Gentle Woman said, "Everything looks as if you were expecting us."

"I have been waiting and hoping for many days," Strong Man replied. "Some families slipped away and came home from Bear Spring. I have talked with them. When I heard you had returned to Fort Defiance, I wanted to come for you, but was afraid to leave the hogan and corrals I have worked so hard to rebuild. Everyone is in such great need, I was afraid our food and the few animals I have would be stolen."

While they were eating, Kee asked, "My father, where have you been all the time we have been prisoners at Bosque Redondo?"

"I have been hiding in the Chuska Mountains. After warning the Diné in the canyon as Long Earrings asked me to that night, I found myself near one of the hidden trails known only to Navajos. I thought if I could find a hideout perhaps I could come back for the rest of you and we could all escape the soldiers. But they moved too swiftly for me. A few families who were already hidden in the mountains and some men who escaped like me, are all the Navajos I have seen until this summer. Blue Cloud brought word to me that you had gone to Fort Defiance. Now I am ashamed I did not come back and look after my family.''

Gentle Woman reached out and put her hand over Strong Man's. "You did what you thought was best. That is all anyone can do.''

"I made it hard for all of you." Strong Man looked at Kee. "My son left here a small boy. He has grown into a man taking care of all of you. When I went raiding I promised him a horse, but he brings home his own horse.''

"My father, you must know by now our tribe has signed a treaty with the government. We are not to raid, nor steal, nor kill. We have promised.''

Wise One shook her finger at Strong Man. "We must keep that promise to our dying breath. We have learned it is possible to get along with the white man.''

Hasba spoke. "Kee has learned to speak the white man's language. I can even say a few words.''

"I went to school at the fort," Kee said. "The government is going to have schools for us here. When the first one is started at Fort Defiance, I would like to go, Father. The more we know of the white man's ways the better it will be for our tribe, I think.''

Strong Man nodded his head. "While you have been away I have had much time to think in loneliness. I am ready to help keep the peace.''

Again, Wise One shook her finger at her son. "I shall remind you of that promise if ever I see the gleam of raiding come into your eyes.''

Strong Man smiled. "That reminds me, my mother, I have a present for you. Come to the sheep corral.''

They all went to the corral to see the present. When the bars were let down, Gray Dog ran Hasba's three sheep inside to join three others and a goat Strong Man had acquired since his return to the mesa.

Taking Wise One to a shelter he had built at the far side of the corral, Strong Man told her to look in. She started to click her tongue. Kee ran to look. Not since Small Burro was drowned had he heard his grandmother click her tongue. Looking over her shoulder, Kee saw the smallest burro he had ever seen. Wise One sat on the ground holding the burro's head in her lap. She stroked his head and long ears. For the second time, Kee saw his grandmother really cry. This time it was for joy.

Gentle Woman laughed. "He is the smallest and nearest to white I have ever seen. Where did you get him?"

"Blue Cloud had a pair of burros he stole from a Mexican ranch. This is their foal. I gave two full-grown goats for this baby because I heard what happened to Small Burro. He is a bit wild, but Grandmother will tame him."

Little Mare began to whinny in the next enclosure. Kee ran to her. He petted his horse and watched sun-bearer prepare to leave the winter sky in a blaze of glory. Everything was touched with a rosy glow—sky, sand, and patches of snow under the trees. Much as he had missed the desert, Kee decided he had not remembered how truly beautiful it was. The quiet was glorious. He could hear only sounds he loved, the subdued voices of his family, and noises made by contented animals moving in their corrals. Peace settled over him. Not since he had left the mesa had he thought of the Blessing Way Chant. Now a verse came to mind and he sang:

"With beauty before me, I walk.
With beauty behind me, I walk.
With beauty all around me, I walk.
In beauty I walk.
In beauty it is finished."

About the Author

Nancy M. Armstrong was born in Yorkshire, England and emigrated to Utah in 1910. She has published over 400 articles and stories.

If you liked *Navajo Long Walk*, you'll like other books in The Council for Indian Education Series. Roberts Rinehart publishes books for all ages, both fiction and non-fiction, in the subjects of natural and cultural history. For more information about all of our books, please write or call for a catalog.

Roberts Rinehart Publishers
P.O. Box 666
Niwot, CO 80544

1-800-352-1985